THE WITCH WHO SAW A STAR

PIXIE POINT BAY BOOK 2

EMMA BELMONT

EMMA ONLINE

Emma loves hearing from her readers!

You can contact her at the links below.

Website: emmabelmont.com

Newsletter: emmabelmont.com/newsletter

Thanks!

1

———

Maris Seaver looked at her watch and frowned. Despite the fog that surrounded the optics room of the lighthouse, she had expected to hear Slick's boat as he went by. Yet, at the appointed time when the three short toots of the horn would have sounded, she had heard nothing.

Could I have missed him?

Slick and *Seas the Day*, his commercial fishing boat, were as punctual as Big Ben and as consistent as the rise of the sun. Nor did the fog deter him. Water was second-nature to the elderly mariner. He'd been boating in Pixie Point Bay, and the ocean beyond, for decades. Although the Old Girl's beam was circling up above as it always did, Maris knew he didn't need it.

She brought the watch to her ear—it was ticking. Once again she peered out into the soupy white mist but the view of the bay was completely obscured. Only the lighthouse's small dock and the rocks directly below were visible.

I must have missed him.

As she checked the time yet again, she realized how late the hour was becoming. She had a B&B to run, and it was time—past time—to get back to it. With a sigh, she reluctantly turned away from the bay.

But as she passed the fresnel lens, she gave its base a gentle pat and said, "Keep an eye out for him, Claribel." If anyone could, it was the magical lighthouse.

Maris made her way down the spiral metal staircase and exited the conical white tower, choosing to walk down the side of the two-story Victorian home. The cool and salty mist enveloped her, and she could hear the waves on the rocks below the point. She mounted the steps to the back porch, passed through its vestibule and the front rooms, and followed her nose.

"What smells like heaven?" Maris asked, as she entered the kitchen. Cookie was at the stove.

"Just a little something I whipped up," Cookie said, with a smile. She eyed Maris's skirt and heels. "That's a pretty combination."

Like her Aunt Glenda, Maris favored skirts, low heels, and frilly blouses. Today she was dressed in a cornflower blue layered skirt, matching open-toed shoes, and a ruffled white blouse.

Ruth "Cookie" Calderon was wearing a short-sleeved cotton dress with her usual large, bright floral print, though it was mostly covered with an apron.

"Thank you," Maris said. "And you're looking your usual vibrant self." She looked over the smaller woman's shoulder. French toast was turning a golden brown in one of the skillets and she could see that Cookie was using her own homemade Italian panettone as the bread. "Genius," Maris said, her mouth watering at the wonderfully sweet scent. "What can I do to help?"

Though Maris wasn't sure, she thought Cookie hesitated.

After twenty-five grinding years in the

hospitality industry, Maris pitched in wherever she could at the B&B, almost out of habit. But she also didn't want the seventy year old chef overdoing it. With shoulder length, salt and pepper hair that was more salt than pepper these days, Cookie had been at the B&B with Maris's aunt for decades.

"Eggs, sunny side up, are on the menu today," the older woman said. "And sliced almond bread for toast."

"I'm on it," Maris said.

She took one of the skillets standing by, lit a burner for it, and set it in place. After she added the butter, she went to the egg basket and fetched three fresh eggs. As she waited for the butter to melt, she unwrapped the loaf of almond bread.

Seeing that the butter was beginning to sizzle, Maris turned down the heat, picked up an egg and cracked it on the edge of the iron skillet. But as she opened it over the pan, a tiny bit of shell fell with the raw egg.

"*Rats*," she said, looking around for something to fetch it out. She spotted the butter knife. But the shell was under the egg white, which was already cooking. As she tried to scrape it to the edge, she accidentally hit the yolk, which began to run. "*Rats.*"

"Over hard," Cookie said calmly. "I like eggs that way as well."

Maris looked at her, and Cookie must have realized she didn't understand. With a deft movement, she used the spatula already in her hand and flipped the egg over. Now the shell was on top. She held her hand out for the butter knife, and used it to flick the bit of shell onto the counter.

"Never crack an egg on the edge of the pan or a bowl," she said quietly, as she picked one up. "You basically force the broken shell up into the egg." She held it over the cutting board on the counter. "Always on the side, against something flat." Using just one hand, she cracked it, took it to the pan, and opened it. A perfectly whole yolk landed in the middle of the white, without a trace of shell. By now the first egg was done, and Cookie moved that to a waiting plate. She smiled at Maris. "Your turn."

But no matter how hard she tried, Maris simply couldn't keep from breaking the yolk: they caught on the shell; the yolk landed too hard; she even dropped the broken shell halves on top of one. She eyed the egg basket and how many were left.

"Shall I finish that?" Cookie asked, apparently seeing the same thing.

By the time Maris looked up from her collection of ruined eggs, the French toast and hash browns were in their warming trays—all done. Maris blinked at them.

Cookie moved the egg skillet to her side of the stove. "The warming trays are ready if you want to take those out."

It was time to admit defeat. "I'd be glad to," Maris said, which was completely true.

One by one she took them to the dining room, then the maple syrup, and the freshly squeezed orange juice in its pretty glass decanter. Back in the kitchen she filled the carafe with fresh coffee, brought it to the sideboard, and made sure the hot water dispenser was hot.

When she returned to the kitchen to wait for the eggs, she said, "By the way, I didn't hear Slick this morning. I'm sure I'm just a worrywart, and he's just taking a day off, but I thought it was strange."

Cookie snorted. "Slick doesn't take days off. He lives to fish, and he knows that most of the restaurants in Pixie Point Bay rely on him for their fresh seafood. More than a few places would be hard pressed to serve meals if he decided to take a few 'days off'."

Hard pressed to serve meals? It wasn't like Cookie to exaggerate, but did Slick really bring in that much fresh catch?

"Whatever the reason, I didn't hear him today." She shook her head and grimaced a little. "Hopefully he came by earlier or later than usual."

Cookie took two china teacups from the cupboard. "How about some tea?" the chef asked.

Although Maris's magic gift, like her aunt's, was precognition, Cookie's was making potions. If she made tea, you could rest assured it was just what you needed.

Maris smiled at her. "Do you have an anti-worrywart tea?"

Cookie gave her a mischievous grin. "I might. We can have it with our eggs." As she steeped their tea in a lovely china pot decorated with bouquets, she said, "I checked the cheeses so I could include some in tomorrow's breakfast, but we might be running a bit low."

Maris went to the stainless steel, double door fridge, and pulled out one of the clear drawers. "We could definitely do with a run to Cheeseman Village," she agreed. "I'll do that today."

The B&B's landline telephone rang just then, making both Maris and Cookie look at the time on the microwave. It was a bit early to call for a reservation but, then again, sometimes people called from faraway time zones. Maris went to the library and picked up the handset of the antique rotary phone.

"Pixie Point Bay Lighthouse and B&B," she said pleasantly. "How can I help you?"

"By coming to the pier," a familiar voice said.

"Slick?" Maris exclaimed. "Is that you? Are you all right?"

Cookie stood at the entry to the library and they exchanged worried looks.

"I'm fine," he said, and Maris let the breath she'd been holding go. She gave Cookie the okay sign, who put a hand over her heart and smiled.

"When I didn't hear your horn this morning," Maris said, "I started to worry."

"You can still worry," Slick replied. "I'm afraid I need a favor."

Maris's eyebrows drew together. "Anything," she said. "Just name it.

"I wonder if you could come to the pier."

"The pier?" Maris looked over at Cookie, who was vigorously nodding and shooing her with one hand. "Of course. I can leave right now. Can you tell me what this is about?"

Slick was silent for a few moments before he said, "There's been a murder." He paused again. "On my boat."

2

———

On any other day at the Pixie Point Bay Pier, Maris loved the smell of the salt air and the frenetic atmosphere created by the mingling of the fishermen and tourists. More than one out-of-town visitor looked over the catch of the day, and decided where to eat based on the haul. But today she couldn't take the time to linger. Instead she went directly to where she knew *Seas the Day* would be docked.

Onboard, she saw Sheriff Mac McKenna and someone she presumed to be a coroner bending over a man's body on the deck. She gasped, and realized that somehow she'd been hoping that Slick was wrong. Another man wearing gloves was snapping photos.

"Thanks for traveling at a rate of knots," a

raspy voice said behind her, and Maris jumped. "I hope you drove safely."

"Slick," she exclaimed as she turned. She embraced him in a hug, which he gently returned. Though tall and wiry, the old mariner had a strength born from decades of hard physical labor. "Are you all right?" she asked.

"Ship shape," he said, letting her go. He wore his signature yellow slicker with matching hat. "It takes more than a dead body to rattle a Duff." His sea green eyes sparkled under thick white brows that matched his long beard.

Maris glanced behind her to the fishing boat. "Who died?"

"Captain––if you can call him that–– Gregory Hazelwood of the *Copernicus*." Slick spoke the words with unvarnished contempt, and nodded at the immense yacht docked next to his vessel. "Worst sailor to ever skim the waters of Pixie Point Bay."

Maris looked over at the enormous white yacht. A gloved forensic technician was working at the railing, at a spot just above where the body lay on *Seas the Day*. There were evidence bags of various shapes and sizes everywhere.

"How did he get on your boat?" she asked. "Did you know each other?"

Slick shook his head. "No. I mean, I recognize the man and that thing he calls a boat, but he's not a real sailor, so we kept our distance from each other."

"I see," Maris said, watching Mac confer with the coroner. "And yet they found him on your boat."

Slick nodded. "That'd be enough trouble for one morning. But I'm afraid that they're going to think that I did it."

Maris's eyebrows drew together. "Why would they think that?" she asked. *Other than the fact that the body is on your boat.*

"On account of the murder weapon," he admitted.

"Which was?" she asked, almost afraid to hear the answer.

"I'm guessing the cause of death was a flare gun," Slick said.

Maris scowled. "A flare gun?" She glanced at the body. "I wouldn't even think that'd be possible."

He took a pipe from his raincoat pocket.

"Yup, me either." He lit the pipe and took a few puffs.

Maris waited for him to continue and, when he didn't, she said, "Then why would you say it was a flare gun?"

He took another puff before withdrawing the pipe. "Because I found it on my deck," he said and paused, casting his gaze to the wide planks of the dock. Then he mumbled something indistinct.

"I'm sorry," Maris said, leaning closer. "What was that?"

He mumbled again, barely audible.

"Slick, you'll have to speak up, I can't–"

"And I picked it up," he almost yelled, and leveled his gaze at her. He quickly put the pipe back in his mouth and clamped down on it.

"Slick," Maris moaned. "You picked it up? Haven't you watched any crime shows? You never pick up the murder weapon."

"In my own defense, I saw the flare gun first," he replied, pointing to *Seas the Day* with his pipe. "It was on the deck over there. I picked it up so I could stow it, and that's when I saw the body."

"So the murder weapon was your flare gun?" Maris asked. That would not be good.

Slick shrugged. "I don't rightly know. The police came before I could look for mine, and booted me off my own boat."

Maris glanced at Mac and the coroner, who were still bent over the body. She wondered what was taking them so long. If Slick was right and Hazelwood had been shot with a flare gun, you'd think the cause of death would be obvious.

"If they think I did it," Slick said, "they're taking the wrong tack." He took a puff on his pipe. "Plenty of the boaters here disliked Hazelwood. He was a poor sailor, despite his background."

"His background?" Maris asked.

"The Navy," the old man replied. "But retired now. Scuttlebutt is that he tried to run that yacht like a ship of war." Slick chuckled a little. "But all you had to know was some math to figure out he'd never served in war time." He puffed on his pipe and seemed to remember something. "Did you ever hear about the time that *Copernicus* nearly cut *Seas the Day* in half?"

Maris doubted if an actual answer to the

question would change the fact that Slick was about to regale her with one of his tall sea tales. She smiled a little as he began.

"It was four summers ago when I was out following a school of salmon. Big one too. Nearly half a nautical mile wide." Maris scowled. A school of salmon that big would have to be as many as there were along the entire coast. "I don't mind telling you that school would have been a good deal smaller once I was done with it." He nodded to himself and took a puff on the pipe. "Clear sky, calm seas, and nigh unto a hundred mile visibility. I was hauling in a good catch, when I looked up to see *Copernicus* bearing down on me. Hazelwood gave that giant horn of his a few long blows, but didn't change course. I had to leave the net and just barely had time to steer the ship out of the way. The fool came within five feet of me and I nearly went into the drink. Lost most of that haul. You'd never seen such happy salmon." He grinned a little at the memory, and took another puff. "Even so I managed to salvage enough of the catch to set a record for the pier. Most fish caught in a day. Record still stands." He took another few puffs and eyed her. "But I didn't ask you here so you could listen to me spin a yarn about the tons that got away."

"No," Maris agreed, "I expect you didn't."

Slick put a hand on her shoulder. "You can get to the bottom of this, just like you did with your Aunt Glenda's death, and the murder of that credit union manager. You follow your heading, Maris, and I know you'll find the truth."

Mac and the coroner had finished their inspection, and the sheriff was leaving the boat.

Maris put her hand over his. "I'll do everything I can, and I'll start by seeing the sheriff."

3

Maris left Slick on the pier and met Mac on the gangway. "Good morning, Mac," she said smiling. He was in full uniform, wearing a khaki long-sleeved shirt that was crisply pressed. His matching trousers had a brown stripe down the sides, the same color as his tie. Above the breast pocket was a name tag and over that a gold badge in the shape of a six-pointed star. The patch on the sleeve was the same shape and read "Medio County Sheriff." He must have left his campaign hat in the car.

"Maris," he said, smiling warmly back at her, "it's good to see you, as always. What brings you here?"

She looked over his shoulder at *Seas the*

Day. "A certain body on a certain friend's boat."

He glanced up at the pier where Slick was smoking his pipe. "Of course," he said, as if remembering. "I know that you and Slick are close."

At Slick's request, and to honor her aunt's wishes as well, she'd never told anyone what the elderly fisherman had confided to her: that he and her aunt had been in a secret relationship. It had charmed her that they'd had each other, and it had also comforted her to have someone else that she could grieve with. Mac knew that the elderly fisherman held a special place in her heart, and he'd simply left it at that.

"Slick called me this morning and asked for my help."

A corner of Mac's mouth crooked up. "That was smart of him." He motioned for her to precede him up the gangway. "We need to let the coroner do his work." Up at the pier again, Slick had fallen into conversation with one of the men fishing from the other side of the pier.

"How much has he told you?" Mac asked.

"I don't suppose he confessed to you that he killed that yacht captain."

For a moment she thought of Slick's tale of nearly being run over, and decided that could wait for another time.

"Really, he's told me very little," she said. "Only that he saw the flare gun first, assumed it was his, and picked it up so he could put it away. Then he saw the body."

"Captain Gregory Hazelwood," Mac said. "Now he's 'ferried o'er death's dark stream'."

"Burns?" Maris asked, knowing Mac's penchant for the Scottish poet.

The sheriff nodded. "He certainly saw his share of death—and then some." He took a notepad from his breast pocket. "I don't have much at this point either." He flipped through a few pages. "The *Copernicus* arrived yesterday and berthed at the pier before the guests left to visit Pixie Point Bay. A few of the crew went out to eat, and one went shopping." He closed the notepad and looked over at the enormous yacht. "I want to solve this one quickly, before the paparazzi land on our doorstep."

The paparazzi? "Who are the guests? Anyone I might have heard of?"

He nodded. "Fritz Falschung, the director, was on board." Maris's eyebrows flew up as she regarded the luxury boat in a new light. "Kaitlyn Cameron, she's an actress. I don't recognize her name. There's also a cine-matographer, and I have yet to question any of them."

Though Maris's hospitality career and the constant moves hadn't left her much free time, she'd certainly heard of the director, and had actually seen a movie with the actress.

"I'll recognize both Falschung and Kait-lyn. She's beautiful."

Mac shrugged, and Maris wondered what Mac *did* look for in a woman. Obviously not young, thin, and pretty.

"Who else was on the yacht?" she asked, gazing at it. The vessel was easily three times the length of Slick's fishing boat. "It doesn't navigate itself—or maybe it does. I wouldn't be too sure these days."

Mac chuckled. "I hear you, but there are five crewmen, not including the captain."

There was a rustling sound from *Seas the Day*. The coroner was covering the body with what looked like a sheet of white plastic.

"What about the murder weapon?" Maris asked. "A flare gun?"

"Yes," Mac acknowledged. "That's a new one for me—thankfully. Turns out it's a pretty grim way to go. He was shot in the back with a flare sometime between yesterday evening, when the yacht arrived, and this morning when the body was spotted—with Slick standing over it."

Maris opened her mouth to ask another question, but she was interrupted by the sound of someone calling her name. The voice startled Maris, because she didn't associate it with Pixie Point Bay or her life here at all. In fact, the voice reminded her of late-night pizza sessions and last minute event planning.

Nadia Malakin stood on the yacht's gangway, wearing a uniform that suggested she worked on the magnificent vessel.

"It is you!" Nadia said, walking down to the platform. "At first, I was sure that I was dreaming. Maris Seaver couldn't possibly be here, in this little town of Pixie Point Bay, but it is you."

"Nadia?" Maris said and headed in her

direction. They met at the bottom of the gangway and hugged. "What in the world?"

"What in the *small* world, I'd say," Nadia said drawing back with a smile. "It's so good to see you."

Maris let her go, grinning back at her. "And you as well."

Apparently life at sea agreed with Maris's former colleague. In her early thirties, slim, with sleek black hair, she was the picture of poise. The smooth, light brown skin of her oval face framed large dark eyes. As she gazed at her, Maris's mind rushed back to those days in the hospitality world, where the pace was grueling and the pressure had been unbearable. She and Nadia could probably spend hours swapping stories, but now was not the time.

"What are you doing here?" Maris asked, though part of the answer was apparent.

"I'm the purser and chief steward of the *Copernicus*," she explained simply. Seeing Maris's look of puzzlement, she added, "I basically run the show, except for driving it. I report—or reported—to the captain." She couldn't help but glance at Slick's boat.

"May I introduce the Medio County sheriff?" Maris said. "Nadia Malakin, this is Sheriff Daniel McKenna. Sheriff, this is a former colleague of mine."

"So I gathered," Mac said, extending his hand, which she shook. "A pleasure."

"Good to meet you," she said, her smile as dazzling as ever.

The last time Maris had seen Nadia, she was managing a trendy and upscale hotel in San Francisco. "How did you end up in boating?"

"Mr. Falschung stayed at the hotel in San Francisco that I was managing. His reservation was a disaster and I took care of it. He offered me twice the salary I was making at the hotel."

"And you left the industry," Maris concluded. That had to have been a no-brainer.

Their attention was drawn to a metallic rattling on the gangway that led from Slick's boat. The coroner and his team were wheeling away the gurney that held the body of Nadia's former boss.

4

The removal of Captain Hazelwood's body put a damper on the reunion. Nadia pointedly looked away from the stretcher and out to the ocean. Though the sheriff watched the coroner and his team, he seemed lost in his thoughts. It was finally Slick, returned from his conversation across the pier, who broke the silence.

"When can I have my boat back?" the old fisherman asked the sheriff.

"It's all clear," Mac said with a nod. "Forensics has gone over everything."

Slick beamed at him. "My thanks, Sheriff."

He'd been about to hurry off, when Mac said, "But I'd like you to stay in port." Slick stopped and turned to stare at him. "I'll be asking the same of the *Copernicus*." Mac leveled his gaze at the old mariner. "It's standard operating procedure."

Though Maris knew that Slick was hardly a flight risk, she also knew that the sheriff couldn't appear to be playing favorites.

"We'll try to be quick," Maris said. She glanced at Nadia. "For everyone's sake."

Though Slick nodded before he turned to go, there was distinctly less spring to his step.

Nadia said, "It would seem we have some time in port." Then she put on a smile and added, "Would you like a tour of the yacht? I'd be happy to show you around."

Maris smiled as well. This was the Nadia she remembered—efficient and also gracious. "I think that would be lovely."

"Thank you," Mac said, "and I'd like to see the owner."

"Of course," Nadia said, easily. "Mr. Falschung should be on-board."

As they approached the yacht, Maris was struck again by how big it was. She looked down the sleek black hull which supported an equally sleek white upper deck. The ship seemed to go on forever.

"It's one-hundred and eighty feet long,"

Nadia said, in answer to Maris's unasked question.

Mac gave a low whistle. "More than half a football field."

Maris recalled what little she'd seen of American football. Her eyebrows raised as she pictured the yacht down on the playing field. It truly was immense.

Fritz Falschung had directed some of the top-grossing films of all-time. The tabloids were full of stories about his opulent lifestyle, lavish parties, and playboy life. But now, seeing the *Copernicus*, Maris understood just how much money might actually be involved.

As they made their way to the boat, Maris saw two figures watching them from the deck. The first she recognized as Kaitlyn Cameron, the actress. Up close, Maris was shocked to see that she was a wisp of a young woman—petite and slim with bright blue eyes and perfectly coiffed shoulder length blonde hair.

The man standing next to her was not an actor. Bespectacled and overweight, his short, mostly gray hair was spiked up in the front, in an attempt to be stylish. He wore an old tweed jacket with patches over the elbows that made him look vaguely scholarly. But a teacher or professor would not be running with this crowd.

Nadia made the introductions. "Kaitlyn Cameron and Alan Hecht," she said gesturing to them. "May I introduce Sheriff McKenna and Maris Seaver—an old friend of mine.

"A sheriff?" Kaitlyn asked, extending her hand to him. "Are you investigating the captain's death?"

"Yes," Mac replied, shaking her hand. "I'll eventually be speaking with everyone on board."

Although Mac seemed nonplussed to be meeting an actual Hollywood actress, Maris found herself a little star struck. In person, Kaitlyn was every bit as pretty as on the screen, if not more so.

"A pleasure," Kaitlyn said, shaking her hand.

"Sheriff," Alan Hecht said, as they shook.

"Mr. Hecht," Mac said. "Are you the cinematographer?"

"I am," he replied, and also shook Maris's hand. "Been with Fritz since the beginning."

Nadia smiled at the two guests. "Have either of you seen Mr. Falschung?"

"Not yet today," Kaitlyn answered.

"Nope," Alan said, then looked over his glasses at the pier and bay. "It's too bad murder-mysteries are out of fashion," he said. "This would be a great setting for a film."

"I'm going to help the sheriff look for Mr. Falschung," Nadia said. "If you see him, please let him know that we're looking for him."

Nadia led them down the length of the yacht, to where a sunken conversation pit was surrounded by a blue and white, leather sectional couch. A set of double doors led into another sitting area replete with bookcases and wall-sized television screens

"The conference room," Nadia said.

A video was playing and, in keeping with the yacht's theme, it appeared to be a drama set at the ocean.

"The dining room," she said, as they passed a lavish room with a stunning teak table and chairs, that had matching wood walls covered in carvings of fish and sea animals.

Though Slick might not have cared for

the captain, Maris thought, he'd approve of the decor.

"Let's see if he's below," Nadia said and motioned to a narrow set of stairs.

As with the dining room, the steps and walls were all covered in teak that had been buffed to a gleaming polish. The hallways of the next level were decorated with enlarged photographs that could have come from the pages of *National Geographic* or *Condé Nast Traveler*. Images of white homes on the island of Mykonos, giant tortoises on the Galapagos, and the seated Egyptian figures at Abu Simbel made Maris wonder if the yacht might have visited all these places.

But the feature that Maris appreciated the most were the windows. Even on this level they were everywhere: letting in natural light, allowing sweeping ocean vistas, and keeping her from feeling like she was in an enclosed space. As they passed an open guest room, Maris noted that the two twin beds had been made with military corners and not a wrinkle to be seen. She nodded in approval. Nadia was obviously seeing to even the smallest of details.

Neither she nor Mac has said a word on

their mini-tour and search. Maris suspected that he was already in investigation mode, while she was busy calculating the extra staff work that it took to maintain these sorts of accommodations.

"The fitness center is this way," Nadia said as she pointed down the hall. "A full set of weights, a Turkish sauna and a jacuzzi for the guests."

At just that moment, the door to the fitness center opened and Fritz Falschung stepped out. He wore a plush purple bath robe and carried a towel and a small electronic tablet. Maris recognized him immediately: the piercing blue eyes, graying hair, and the mostly white and very closely trimmed beard. Despite the robe, the director was also wearing a white captain's hat, set back on his head at a rakish angle.

"Mr. Falschung," Nadia said, "may I introduce an old friend of mine from the hotel days, Maris Seaver."

The director leaned forward slightly, and quickly smiled. "Pleasure."

Despite having met and taken care of her share of celebrities, Maris felt a tremor of nervousness. "Nice to meet you," she finally said.

Nadia turned slightly and said, "This is Daniel McKenna. He's the sheriff for the county, and he's looking into Captain Hazelwood's death."

As the two men shook hands, Fritz said, "Nice to meet you too. We're getting the county sheriff and not the town's? That's rather impressive."

Mac smiled. "Pixie Point Bay doesn't have its own sheriff, so I do double duty."

Falschung nodded thoughtfully. He turned to Maris. "And how long have you known our Nadia?"

"Seven years, maybe?" Maris said. She couldn't count the number of events they'd done together. "It's been a long time."

"Maris is a problem-solver from way back," Nadia said.

"Indeed," Falschung said, "you'll have to tell me about that some time. It sounds fascinating." But the tone of his voice said that it sounded anything but, and Maris felt her smile become forced.

"Well," Nadia said. "I need to see to some duties."

But before she could turn to go, Falschung tossed the towel at her feet. "Put this wherever it goes."

Maris had to blink at the regal tone and nonchalant rudeness. For a moment, she thought she hadn't heard right. But when she glanced at Mac who was frowning at the towel on the floor, she knew she'd heard perfectly. Nadia's pleasant expression remained fixed as she bent and picked up the towel before leaving.

Although Maris would have liked to arrange a meeting with her, or at least thank her for her time, a distinct chill had settled in the little corridor. Based on what Nadia had said about her salary and position, Maris doubted that picking up towels was part of her duties—which meant the little performance had been for their benefit. The famous director was showing Maris and Mac who was the boss.

"I have a few questions I'd like to ask," Mac said.

"Perfect," Fritz said, his expression animated. "Like a noir movie—except for that getup of yours." He gave Mac's brown and tan sheriff's uniform a long look, before he said, "Go ahead."

Maris saw the muscles at Mac's jaw working. "The captain of your boat has just died, and yet you're having a sauna." He took the notepad from his breast pocket. "Murder happen a lot on your boat?"

Maris stiffened a little at the antagonistic tone, but, to her surprise, the director laughed.

"It's a ship," he replied, "not a boat." He eyed them both. "I have a strict sauna routine. Every day, without interruption. It would be a shame if the routine stopped now, and I'm sure Hazelwood wouldn't have wanted me to pause it on his account." Falschung's answer seemed entirely sincere —and completely selfish. Suddenly the handsome playboy was looking distinctly less attractive. "I'll give you a tour of the ship," he said, turning to go.

"Nadia was kind enough to show us the highlights," Mac said. Maris sensed the sheriff's growing irritation and guessed he'd rather just ask questions.

The director stopped and turned. "That's not her responsibility," he declared, scowling.

"She's paid to count my money, not entertain. I'll have to speak to her about that. Have you seen the bridge?"

Mac snapped his notebook closed and was drawing in a breath, when Maris interjected, "No, but we'd love to."

"Good," he said turning away from them. "This way."

Maris gave Mac a sympathetic look, and the sheriff grimaced and shook his head.

Fritz led them back up the stairs to the first deck, and then up another set of stairs to the top of the ship. More gleaming white metal greeted them, but at this level, tinted windows surrounded the single-story structure on all sides.

More than that, the view was tremendous. Maris had never seen the pier from this vantage point. It was almost like being at the top of the lighthouse. But Fritz hadn't paused to take in the surroundings. Instead he opened the door on the side of the superstructure.

As they entered, he grandly gestured around and said, "The wheelhouse."

Maris had to make sure her jaw didn't drop. It was more like the command deck of a space ship than a yacht. Computer screens formed a complete semi-circle at the front, just below the forward facing windows. Various keyboards and controls were at waist level, and two swivel chairs were at either side of the room. Behind everything was the large and elevated captain's chair, with its own consoles of mini-screens and buttons built into its arms.

"Wow," she muttered.

Fritz smiled as he took a seat in the captain's chair, cutting a slightly comedic figure in the hat and robe.

Mac turned to him. "Who would have wanted to see the captain dead?"

Fritz took off the hat, and set it in his lap. "Let's be honest here. I feel like I can talk to you two. The captain was a jerk. Nobody liked him, including me. He had served in the Navy, which I respect, but Hazelwood wanted to pretend that we were all in the service with him. We had to address him as Captain, *even me*. He wouldn't answer if you called him Gregory."

"So he wanted to be addressed by his title," Mac said, taking a few notes. "Anything else?"

Falschung laughed and showed him the

captain's hat. "I was wearing this one night as part of an outfit, and he refused to start the engines until I took it off. I wanted to wear a hat on my own damn ship, and he had the nerve to tell me that I couldn't. I was outraged. I had to take the thing off before we could leave port." He put the hat back on, tugging it firmly down into place.

"Where were you last night?" Mac asked.

"In my cabin."

"Can anyone corroborate your whereabouts?"

"Kaitlyn was with me," Falschung said, smirking. "All night, if you take my meaning."

Maris was now entirely unimpressed with this celebrity. She could care less about who was involved with who, or what they did. But at the same time, his tone set her nerves on edge—he was bragging.

The director sat forward on the chair. "Does this mean I'm a suspect?" he asked, animated again. "This is fabulous." He took out his small tablet and began recording notes to himself. Most of them dealt with how he felt about being a suspect: how he might fear for his freedom, or how he was offended, or if he should run. He also said "based on true events."

Next he'll want to spend some time in a jail cell, Maris thought drily. As she watched Mac's lips press into a thin line, she wondered if the sheriff would oblige him.

"No one is a suspect yet," Mac said. "We're still gathering evidence."

Falschung waved him off with a dismissive gesture, before staring at Mac's utility belt. "Why don't you wear a gun?"

Maris looked at Mac's belt. She'd never noticed whether or not he wore a gun. If anything she'd just assumed that all law enforcement officials did. But as she discreetly raised a couple fingers to her temple and tapped—triggering her photographic memory—she called up images with the sheriff. In none of them did he wear a sidearm.

"Are sheriffs not allowed?" Fritz asked, taking out his tablet again.

"Sheriffs are permitted to carry a sidearm at all times," Mac replied. "I just choose not to."

Falschung gave him an incredulous look. "Why wouldn't you if you could? I know I'd have one with me at all times."

"Their gun's a burden on their shoulder," Mac said.

Although Maris suspected it was a quote from Mac's favorite poet, the director cocked his head at him. "Who's gun?" he asked.

"It's a quote from Robert Burns," Mac said, not elaborating.

A member of the crew carrying a clipboard entered the bridge, saw the three of them, and paused at the threshold.

"Ah," Fritz said. "First Mate Lloyd Kunkel. Looks like you're running the ship now."

"Pardon me, Mr. Falschung," the first mate said. "I didn't realize you were having a meeting."

Before Fritz could answer, Mac said, "We just finished. I wonder if I could ask you a few questions."

The first mate looked caught, glancing between the sheriff and the director.

Fritz got up from the captain's chair and pulled his robe tight around him. "The bridge is yours, first mate." He grinned slyly at Maris. "I've always wanted to say that."

5

Maris breathed a sigh of relief as the director departed. She should have known better than to expect the persona she'd seen in tabloids and sound bites. But she'd never have expected such an egotist.

"I'll need just a minute before we start," the first mate said, and set down the clipboard. "I have to make some log entries."

She and Mac watched as the young officer turned on screens, flipped through columns of data, and what looked like weather charts, only to then copy and paste from one screen to another. In the next instant, he seemed to be looking at some kind of schematic of the ship, and Maris saw a little bar chart where the colored columns rose and fell in real time. Given that the yacht was docked, it was incredible how many systems seemed to be operating—or at least needed to be monitored. She and Mac exchanged impressed looks.

Finally the first mate seemed to be satisfied about the state of the ship, switched off one of the monitors, and turned to them.

"Sorry about that," he said, "it's just part of my rounds."

Maris smiled. "I didn't realize that so much went into running a ship like this. It's like a floating hotel with gauges."

The first mate laughed. "That's a great analogy. I'm Lloyd Kunkel by the way." He held out a hand to Maris and then Mac.

Though Lloyd was bald under the white wheel cap, he looked to be in his early thirties. Trim, tan, and of average height, his hazel eyes were kind and his smile warm.

"How long have you been the first mate on the *Copernicus*?" Mac asked.

He thought for a moment. "About two years," he said. "I hired on in this position."

"And before that?" Mac asked, making a note.

"One year as second mate on the *Atlantia*

out of Rotterdam," he said. "I've come up all the way from deckhand on different ships, starting nine years ago."

Although Lloyd hadn't said so, Maris didn't think he'd come up through the military, like the captain. His uniform was clean and pressed, and he seemed to have gone about his log duties efficiently, but he also had an easy manner about him, which didn't seem particularly military.

"You reported directly to the captain?" Maris asked.

"Exactly," he said. "Both Nadia...I mean Ms. Malakin. Both Ms. Malakin and I are... I'm sorry, *were* direct reports." He took off his hat for a moment, passed a hand over his smooth head, and replaced the cap. "I haven't quite wrapped my head around the fact that he's gone." He fixed his gaze on the captain's chair, narrowing his eyes. "He was sitting there just yesterday." He shook his head.

"Fritz Falschung indicated that the captain was disliked," Mac said, and Maris saw him waiting for Lloyd's reaction.

The first mate grimaced. "He's hardly been dead a day," he muttered looking at the chair. Then he met Mac's gaze. "Captain ran a tight ship, no doubt. He wasn't an easy man to work for but he was fair. The crew works long days on a ship like this. There's bound to be some grousing."

It wasn't the most ringing of endorsements that Maris had ever heard, but Lloyd seemed truly pained to hear that Hazelwood had been disparaged.

"And this grousing," Mac said, "do you think any of the crew took it more seriously?"

Lloyd shook his head. "It's just part of life at sea. Every boat has its share of drama and frayed nerves."

Mac crossed his arms over his chest. "It's more than drama and frayed nerves when someone's killed."

Lloyd spread his hands. "Look, most of the crew didn't interact with the captain. He was old-school, all the way. There was a hierarchy and Captain Hazelwood enforced it. Everything went through myself or Nadia, depending on the issue. He wouldn't have spoken to someone outside the chain of command. The crew only knew him second hand."

Mac made a quick note before asking, "Are all of your flare guns accounted for?"

The first mate's eyes darted to the window behind them, and then at the floor. He picked up his clipboard and took a pen from his pocket. "I'll find out," he said, making a note.

Maris waited for him to finish. "Do you like your job?" she asked, switching topics.

He paused at the sudden change. "It's the best job in the world. I get to do something I love." Now he smiled at Maris as he tucked the clipboard under his arm. "Mr. Falschung loves to travel, and I figure that by the time I hang up my hat, I'll have been around the world two or three times. Not many sailors can say that."

"Where were you at the time of the murder last night?" Mac asked, doing the same quick change that she had.

Lloyd cocked his head and looked at Mac. "You mean you think that I might have killed Captain Hazelwood?" He looked from him to Maris and back again. "I didn't. I was in my room last night, asleep."

"Alone?" Mac asked.

After Falschung's alibi, Maris had to inwardly cringe as she waited for the answer.

"Alone," the first mate affirmed. "The shifts here are typically fourteen hours, with one day off every other week. When I hit my bunk, I just want to sleep."

A soft chime rang throughout the bridge and Lloyd checked his watch. "Lunchtime. You're more than welcome to stay. The chef puts on a spread like you wouldn't believe."

Maris had no doubt that was true, given the opulent surroundings and Nadia managing. She might even learn a thing or two about the guests or how the ship was run. But she had her own B&B, and needed to make a run to Cheeseman Village as well.

Mac smiled his thanks as he tucked his notepad into his breast pocket. "I'm going to meet with the coroner."

When the first mate looked at Maris, she said, "Artisanal cheese waits for no man." Although she laughed a little, neither of the men did. She cleared her throat. "I've got to make a supply run for the B&B."

"Another time, then," Lloyd said.

"Perhaps," Mac said, "because I'll need you to stay in port until we've established more facts about the death, and I've had a chance to talk with everyone on-board."

The first mate glanced at the captain's chair, as though he was expecting a countermanding order, but finally said, "Understood."

"It's standard operating procedure," Mac said as he headed to the door. As Maris followed him, he opened it for her. "But I'll make it as quick as possible. We'll be back at..." He gave Maris a look. "Nine a.m.?"

When she nodded, the sheriff looked at Lloyd, who also nodded. "I'm sure we'd all appreciate it."

Maris set up her GPS and, from the Pixie Point Bay Pier, took the dramatic and scenic highway north. Where it skirted the coastline, the view to the rocks below was dizzying. Buff cliffs surrounded much of the bay and, at this time of day, they were undulating curtains of dusky terra cotta ringing a sparkling turquoise basin.

The view from the Pixie Point Bridge was equally impressive, including the bridge itself. It's high stone arches rounded upward from the sides of the deep ravine that it crossed. A small river flowed far below, winding its way to a small estuary. Even from this elevation, Maris could make out the blue dots of tide pools around its craggy rim.

Although Maris had her fears—to be sure—heights was thankfully not one of them.

One of these days, she vowed to herself, *I'm going to park this car and have a good, long look.*

As the panoramic drive wound inland, she passed through the grassy rolling hills that surrounded Cheeseman Village. The dairy's black and white cows dotted the landscape, heads down, cropping the sweet countryside. A few were lying down under the shade of the occasional oaks. Some even seemed to be running after one another and cavorting. As the cows became more dense, she began to pass some barns as well, before entering the village proper.

Small, single-story homes with mailboxes on the two-lane highway began to appear, eventually giving way to larger tracts of houses. But the suburban outskirts of Cheeseman Village didn't sprawl. Despite the huge acreage devoted to the herds, the village itself was compact. In no time, following the GPS directions, Maris found herself in a pleasant downtown district where the cars all parked at a diagonal to the sidewalk in front of colorful shops. Finally though, at the town's center, she arrived at the Cheeseman Village Dairy.

Despite the last century feel of the surrounding area, the dairy itself was a thoroughly modern building. It's slanted metal roof rested on two-story high windows all around. As Maris parked the car and got out, she decided that it was more than a dairy—it was also a welcome center and it certainly looked the part.

As the glass entry doors slid open, a young woman with a tray of cheese cubes greeted her.

"Welcome to the Cheeseman Village Dairy," she said, wearing jeans, a bright yellow polo shirt that sported the dairy's two-cow logo, and a matching baseball cap. "Would you care to sample some cheese?"

Maris could already feel her stomach rumbling. After dashing out to the pier before breakfast and lunchtime rolling by on the yacht, she was ready for something—anything. She stepped right up to the tray. It looked like a scrumptious selection.

The young woman pointed with a gloved hand. "Cheddar, Gouda, Monterey Jack, Muenster, and Colby."

Using the toothpicks from the cow-shaped holder built into the tray, Maris quickly made her selection. "Gouda," she said, spearing a cube. "The gateway cheese to the world of the artisanal. And Muenster, and Colby." The flavorful cheeses were her favorites. "I'll start with these," she said.

The young woman beamed at her. "Excellent choices. You know your cheese."

Maris patted her tummy with her free hand. "A little too well," she said.

"Please let any of the associates on the floor know if you have any questions," she said cheerily, as Maris turned to head into the store.

"I'll do that," Maris said, and popped the Muenster in her mouth and almost rolled her eyes. It was perfect—with its smooth texture and the lovely, sweet, and nutty flavor of its bright orange rind. She would be picking up some Muenster for sure.

She picked up a store shopping basket, and went on the hunt. It wasn't the first time she'd shopped at the dairy, but the choices were mind-numbing. The market took up the entire floor of the building, with refrigerated cases as far as the eye could see. On the second level, at the back of the expansive room, there was a loft. Maris knew from the signs near the stairs that it held an observation deck that looked down on part of the packaging plant. Like the drive over the bridge, she promised herself that one day she'd make time to go up there. If nothing else, it might be something that the B&B guests would be interested in seeing. But Maris knew she couldn't recommend something unless she'd seen it, heard it, tasted it, or done it. It had long been a hospitality rule of her own making.

As she munched on the rest of her samples, she perused the longest cheese case in the market. Artfully arranged, it was organized in no particular order, or at least none that she could discern. With an eye toward wine pairings, accompanied by crackers, bread, nuts, and fruits, she let her creativity reign. When she spotted a cheese that appealed, she simply picked it up, trusting her instincts. At the age of fifty, including twenty-five years of wine and cheese boards, they were instincts that were finely honed.

In the middle of the market were islands of goods that were obviously grouped. At each one she made a stop, picking up savory crackers at the first, pretzel sticks at another, dried fruit at yet another, and finally some brown mustard. She'd have to tell Nadia about the dairy. No doubt the yacht's galley was fully stocked, but the dairy might provide a nice change of pace.

Thinking of her former colleague, Maris couldn't help but remember the way Falschung had treated her. Even now it made her angry, along with him bragging about his conquest. He'd also told them that the captain had been roundly disliked. But their conversation with the first mate hadn't confirmed that.

Maris could easily see how the director and the captain would have been at loggerheads. But the question was: enough for murder?

"Uh oh," she muttered, as she looked up to find herself in the ice cream aisle.

Her chocolate-finding superpower had unerringly led her directly to the triple fudge ice cream. The image on the carton used the two-cow logo standing next to a small mountain of luscious brown ice cream scoops, sitting in the landscape of the surrounding green hills. Maris knew only too well that little cubes of fudge brownie were hidden within the scoops. Although she gazed at the container for another long few seconds, she made herself step away. Today she was winning the battle of the bulge.

But as she headed toward the checkout stands, her surroundings vanished and she came to an abrupt stop. By now Maris understood that her magical gift was taking over. Like her aunt, she'd been blessed with the ability of precognition. When her vision returned, she wasn't surprised to find that she no longer saw the dairy. Instead, she saw a boat. In fact, she was on it. As she took in the details, she realized it was *Seas the Day*, although Slick was nowhere in sight. But along with the vision came the scents of the scene as well. Maris frowned when her nose was greeted by an astringent odor instead of the briny smell of the sea. Though she didn't associate it with the pier, Maris knew that smell —from hotels under renovation.

"Turpentine," she muttered.

Suddenly, the dairy popped back into view.

As usual with her magic ability, she didn't

know quite what to make of it. That the vi-sion had to do with the murder, she had no doubt, especially since it had been on Slick's boat. But for now she would have to trust that the meaning of the turpentine would become clear later.

She checked her basket of goods and then headed to the cash registers.

7

Maris pulled into one of the manicured gravel parking slots in front of the B&B, alongside an SUV which she knew belonged to the Magnusons, a retired couple staying as guests. She managed to bring in both bags from the dairy at once and took them directly to the kitchen. The cheese went into the big refrigerator, but the other goods went into the B&B's larder.

Like the traditionally styled kitchen, the quaint charm of the larder was only a facade. Beneath the traditional curved coves that connected the walls to the ceiling, and the decorative plaster medallions overhead, the pantry was all business. The rolling shelves were shallow enough to allow a view of all the essentials. Drawers at their bottoms were fronted with clear plexiglass for the same reason. Spice cabinets folded out from the walls and a glass and metal wine refrigerator occupied the far end. Maris took care to store her goods according to Cookie's very organized scheme.

Once that was done, she peeked out the back porch door and saw the chef in the herb garden, as she was most every afternoon. But as voices drifted to her from the hallway, Maris wandered in their direction. In the parlor she found the Magnuson's, Gayle and Mark, together on the green velvet divan and Mojo curled up on the ottoman. The small but slightly pudgy black cat was apparently enjoying the company and his afternoon siesta.

"Good afternoon," Maris said with her usual cheer.

They looked up from the camera that Gayle held in her hands, already smiling. Maris guessed them both in their early seventies, though their trim fitness and the walking outfits certainly belied their age. Mark was easily over six feet tall, and Gayle wasn't much shorter.

"Well hello, Maris," Gayle said, and Mark said, "Hi there."

"You two look like you've been for a walk," Maris said, going to the ottoman. "Did you enjoy it?" She stroked Mojo's soft and fluffy flank.

"It was *wonderful*," Gayle said. "We ventured inland today and visited the redwoods. Simply gorgeous."

As Mojo raised his head to look at her, Maris crouched next to the ottoman. "Did you walk the Secoya Trail?"

"Yep," Mark said. "Just like you told us. We left the car at the trailhead, already surrounded by the forest."

Maris had done some small morning and afternoon hikes there, not as long as the ones she'd done as a girl. But without much elevation gain, it was ideal if you simply wanted to stroll among the massive and majestic trees. Even at the trailhead, the redwood forest was so thick, you could hardly see the sky.

"Of course I'd seen photographs of them," Gayle said. "But the real things...well, they take your breath away."

Maris knew from previous chats with them that Mark had retired from a dot-com startup in Portland and Gayle had been a professional photographer.

"Well, that and the long walk," Mark said, laughing a little. "That took my breath away too."

Gayle flipped a switch on her digital SLR and the screen on the back brightened. She offered it to Maris. "Would you like to see?"

"I'd love it," Maris said, standing and taking the camera from her.

Mojo looked up at her with his glittering orange eyes.

"Just press that little forward arrow button," Gayle said, pointing at it.

But Maris wasn't all that anxious to move on to the next photo. She was still enjoying the first. The nearly crimson tree trunks rose grandly from every edge of the image, their distant green tops almost meeting in the center. Beyond them was a pale blue sky, and dusty sunbeams descending in their midst. Though it fit in the palm of Maris's hand, the photo captured the forest's quiet majesty as though it were a cathedral.

Each image was completely different. Gayle had clearly not been interested in variations on a theme. The brook that flowed beside a section of the path had turned into a milky, time-lagged blur that seemed to float against the mossy green river rocks that bounded it. Next was a closeup of ferns at the base of a tree, their fine leaf points spotlighted by a bright sliver of sun. Maris had to force herself to stop.

She shook her head as she handed the camera back. "These are stunning, Gayle. Absolutely stunning. Any one of these could be hanging in a gallery."

Gayle took the compliment in stride, and gave Maris a little smile. "Thank you."

Mark put an arm around his wife's shoulders. "That's my little shutterbug," he said, and gave her a peck on the cheek that really made her smile.

Maris simply grinned and watched them for a moment before she said, "I hope that you got some refreshments when you returned home." She nodded at the camera. "It looks to me like you covered quite a bit of ground."

Mark smiled up at her. "We did. Cookie brought us some tea that was made from herbs straight from the garden."

"I don't think I've ever had garden-fresh

tea like that," Gayle said. "It was so refreshing that I feel ready for another hike." Mark quickly nodded in agreement, and Maris noted that they truly did look invigorated.

Maris had to hand it to the petite potion-maker and chef. Whatever had been in the tea had done the trick.

"Would you look at that," Gayle said as she got up, set aside her camera, and went to the Victorian writing table. She picked up the Ouija board. "I haven't seen one of these since I was a kid."

Mojo gave a meow that did his namesake proud, and sounded like a tiny, tinny harmonica. Maris's Aunt Glenda had named him after a famous blues harmonica player.

Mark laughed. "Well *someone* wants to see that board."

Gayle brought the board and plastic planchette to the coffee table and set it down. Mojo immediately jumped down from the ottoman and up next to the board.

"So what should we ask?" Mark said.

Gayle smiled and clapped her hands together as she took a seat beside him. "I know." She turned to Maris. "Our third grandchild will be born next month, but the parents don't want to know if it's a boy or a girl." She turned to Mark. "Let's ask the Ouija board."

Mark grinned at her. "Good choice." They both placed their fingers gently on the edge of the planchette.

"Spirit of the Ouija board," Mark intoned, "will our grandchild be a boy or a girl?"

Mojo put a single paw on the planchette with them. "Look at that," Gayle said, obviously delighted. "Mojo wants to know too."

They didn't have to wait for long, as the planchette began to move. Although the Magnusons seemed oblivious to Mojo's expression as they stared at the board, Maris could see that his amber eyes seemed to have focused on something far away. His ears swiveled in near full circles, like tiny radar dishes.

"Y," Mark said, as the planchette's clear window passed over that letter.

"A," Gayle said, looking perplexed. "C," she said as the letter quickly followed.

Mark added, "H."

Maris felt a tingling shiver down her spine. Mojo was spelling the word "yacht."

"T," Gayle said, as the planchette came to

a stop. She looked up at Mark. "Our grand-child is a boat."

"As long as he or she is a healthy boat," Mark said with a smile. "Let's try this one more time." He pushed the planchette back to the start.

"I'd settle for a dinghy this time," Gayle said with a smile. But then she took on a mock serious look and tone. "Tell us the sex of our next grandchild."

The planchette wobbled and then slid to "Y" again. Gayle shot her husband a look. "Will you stop that? You've been bugging me for a boat for ages, but I want to know about the baby, not what you want for our an-niversary."

He laughed again and lifted his hands in the air. "There. Now you know it's not me."

But to both of their amazements, she and Mojo spelled "yacht" yet again.

Gayle stared down at the board as Mojo shook out his fur, leapt to the ground, and bounced out into the hallway without so much as a look back.

Maris looked at the planchette still over the last letter. Twice, Mojo had spelled yacht, but how did that help her? She already knew that the murderer was likely someone on the *Copernicus*, since it couldn't be Slick. Frankly, she already thought she knew who it was. How did seeing the word "yacht" help?

She headed to the doorway but paused. "Is there anything I can get for you?" Maris asked the couple.

Mark had picked up the planchette and was examining its underside. Gayle was still staring at the board, but finally seemed to have heard.

"Oh, no, Maris," she said, glancing at her. Mark put the planchette back on the board. "But thank you."

"All right," Maris said. "Wine and cheese as usual later."

Neither of them replied, but instead had placed their fingers on the planchette again.

Maris had to grin a little. She'd probably have to serve the wine and cheese in here.

8

———

The next day, after the morning breakfast routine, Maris had made the foggy drive to the pier to meet Mac. Her tires bumped rhythmically over the giant planks of the dock as she made her way to the end of the parking lot. Unlike yesterday, with the emergency vehicles and the local fisherman looking on, this morning the pier was quiet.

White mist enshrouded the working end of the long wharf, where the buildings that were used to store equipment and process catch were located. No sound came from them, nor did there seem to be any boat traffic. Only a few fisherman had their lines dropped over the side into the glassy water, compared to the dozens she'd seen yesterday.

As she made her way past the first two, she peeked inside their buckets: nothing. She frowned a little. Neither had caught a single thing. That had to be a new record, of a sort, for the pier. No wonder no one was here. But as she came up to the final fisherman, she recognized his young face when he pulled back the hoodie.

"Good morning, Ryan," she said, glancing down into his bucket. He'd caught a single flounder, though it was a good size.

"Top of the morning," he replied, "though not exactly good."

His fiery red hair was pulled back in a sleek pony tail, contrasting with the tranquil green glow of his eyes and the paleness of his complexion. This was not the first time Maris had run across the owner of Castaways, the tackle shop in town, fishing at the pier. But she'd never seen his bucket so empty. On a normal day, he seemed to reel in the catches almost non-stop.

She glanced up and down the dock. "Fish not biting today?"

In answer, he eyed his line and cranked the handle on the reel. Maris watched as the nylon thread rose from the water. In a few moments she saw a small, neon-yellow fish on a hook, followed by something that looked like a spinning pompon, also in yellow but with red fringes. They bounced to and fro as Ryan brought them up, followed by a teardrop shaped lead weight.

When they drew closer, Maris could see that the yellow fish were not fish at all, but shaped pieces of rubber. As they approached the tip of the rod, Ryan deftly swung them over the railing and caught the weight in his other hand.

"These are the best artificials you can get," he said, wrapping the weight around the rod. "Top notch lures. They never fail." He pointedly looked in his bucket. "Until today." Then he shrugged and smiled at her. "I'll try again tomorrow. Good things come to those who bait."

As he closed up his tackle box, Maris asked, "Does this happen from time to time? That the fish simply don't seem to bite?"

He gathered up the box and rod in one hand, and the bucket in the other. "Not that I've ever seen." Then he looked down the pier to where *Seas the Day* was docked. "Then again, I've never seen Slick in port for the day either. For all our sakes, I hope he sets sail soon."

Maris's eyebrows drew together as she gazed at Slick's boat. What did that have to do with catching fish here?

"I've got to go open up my shop," the young man said, heading off. "Have a nice day."

"You too," Maris said to his back.

As she approached Slick's boat, she mulled over the strange conversation. Cookie had let her know that it was impolite to inquire directly of another witch, wizard, mage, or any type of magic person regarding their ability. But Maris had suspected from the beginning that both Slick and Ryan were magic folk. The fact that her Aunt Glenda had been involved romantically with the elderly fisherman had been her first clue. Ryan's amazing way with a rod and reel had been her second.

On-board *Seas the Day*, Slick seemed to be busy on deck.

"Good morning," Maris called down to him from the pier.

"Ahoy there," he called back, giving her a wave. He had something in his hand, but he brought it to the prow of the ship so he could be closer.

She squinted down at it. It looked like a bunch of rope. "Are you practicing tying knots?"

"Tying knots, yep," Slick said, surprising her. "But not practicing."

He held up the lines of netting that she'd thought was rope, and spread his hands. In the middle of the widely spaced green mesh was a hole about the size of a basketball.

"Oh," she exclaimed. "That's not good."

Slick shook his head and let most of the net fall back to the deck. "Not unless you're trying to catch sharks."

Then he took a tool from the slicker's pocket that looked to Maris like a weaver's flat shuttle, an implement she associated with a loom, not the deck of a fishing boat. But wound inside its middle was the same green cord that made up the net. True to his word, Slick took a bit of the green cord and tied it to the existing net at the hole, using movements like a surgeon tying off a knot. Once he'd tugged it tight, he used the shuttle like a big needle, threading it through an adjacent part of the net. Then he tied another knot. Loop by loop, he created a row across the top of the hole. In only a few moments, he created a second row of loops under the first, crossing the hole in the opposite direction, and linking it to the first row.

"I guess you've done this before," Maris said, fascinated with the process.

"Yep," he said nodding, but not stopping. "It's the first job I learned on the deck." When he finished the second row, he looked up at her and smiled. "On account of it not being important."

Important or not, Slick was obviously making good use of the time he had to spend in port. As she watched him start the third row, Ryan's words came back to her—*I hope he sets sail soon*. Then she remembered Cookie's words about the restaurants—*hard pressed to serve meals*. There was more to the elderly mariner than just commercial fishing. There had to be. She'd just about worked up enough nerve to ask him, when Mac came up behind her.

"Good morning," he said, giving her a start. As she covered her heart with her hand, he added, "Sorry. I thought you heard me."

"Good morning," she gasped. She'd been

concentrating on Slick so hard that she hadn't heard a thing. "No problem," she said, her breathing returning to normal. "Slick and I were just chatting."

"Looks like it's all hands on deck," Slick called up to the sheriff with a wave. "Any chance I'll be able to fish later today?"

"Not likely, Mr. Duff," Mac said. "But you'll be the first to know."

Mac had turned to go but Slick called out, "Hold on," and disappeared into the wheelhouse. He emerged with what looked like a bright orange tackle box. "Dry emergency storage," he said loudly. Then undid the clasps, opened it and took out a matching orange flare gun. He showed it to the sheriff. "All accounted for."

"Duly noted," Mac called back.

Slick waved his hand in the direction of the giant yacht. "Best get cracking then."

Mac waved back at him as he and Maris headed that way.

"Well, that's a relief," Maris said, "not that I doubted him."

As they mounted the gangway, Mac said, "He could own two." When Maris shot a look at him, he added, "Not that I doubted him either. It's a matter of what holds up in court."

Without anyone on the deck to greet them like yesterday, Mac and Maris simply wandered back along the deck, the way that Nadia had led them. But today, on the aft deck, Alan Hecht, the cinematographer was having breakfast.

Maris couldn't help but take note of the meal—Eggs Benedict, Belgian waffles, and what looked like fresh orange juice. Despite the unexpected layover, Nadia was making sure the guests were taken care of.

"Mr. Hecht," Mac said, causing him to look up in mid-bite. "Sorry to interrupt your breakfast. I'd like to ask you some questions."

Hecht finished that bite and nodded as he wiped his mouth with a linen napkin. He gestured to the sectional couch opposite him. "Of course," he said. "Please, sit down." He'd been reading a tablet of some sort, but turned it off and set it aside. "I've been expecting you."

"Oh?" Maris said, taking a seat.

The cinematographer pushed his plate to the side. "The first mate said you'd be talking with everyone." He smiled at them both. "And please call me Alan."

"Thanks," Mac said as he took a seat too, and brought the notepad from his breast pocket. "How well did you know the captain?"

"Well?" Alan said. "I wouldn't say I knew him at all. He took his orders from Fritz—or at least that's what he'd like to believe."

"How long have you known Fritz?" Maris asked.

Hecht laughed a little. "Longer than I care to remember." He picked up his glass of juice. "Since the beginning, about thirty years ago." He took a sip.

As Mac made a note, Maris said, "Since you're a cinematographer and he's a director, it must have been a good fit."

Hecht laughed again as he set his glass down. "We started as actors, like everybody else—and I do mean everybody."

Although Maris could picture Falschung in front of the screen, she couldn't really imagine Alan as an actor.

At her look of puzzlement, he said, "We were in LA, waiting tables, auditioning for bit parts, when he decided to write his own movie and direct it, so we could star in it." He smiled and shook his head. "Just a couple of kids really. I borrowed someone's camera, and we were off and running."

"And you're still running," Maris said, smiling.

Alan tilted his head. "You can't argue with success. The man has a nose for story. He's a storytelling genius." The cinematographer indicated himself. "Me? I've been along for the ride." He gestured to the surroundings. "And what a ride it is."

"How did Fritz and Captain Hazelwood get along?" Mac asked.

Alan snorted. "Not too well, if you ask me. It's like having two directors on a movie. It doesn't work." But when he realized what he'd said, he quickly added, "Their disagreements were strictly professional. Fritz is many things, but violent is not one of them."

"Where were you at the time of the murder?" the sheriff asked.

"Alone in my cabin," Alan said, "probably asleep." He paused for a moment before asking, "Is it true? Was Hazelwood shot with a flare gun?"

Mac nodded. "He was." Although Alan

waited, as though Mac might elaborate, he didn't—and Maris was glad.

The sound of footsteps drew all their attention to Kaitlyn Cameron. The young actress was holding a plate of fresh fruit, and also a piece of paper.

"Good," she said to Mac. "Now I don't have to go looking for you."

9

While Kaitlyn sat down, Alan got up. "I'll let you get to it," he said to them. "Unless you have more questions for me?" He looked at the sheriff.

"Not for now," Mac said. "Thanks for your time."

The cinematographer picked up his tablet, but left the food, and headed back inside.

"I didn't mean to make him leave," Kaitlyn said, looking after him. Then she moved his plate aside so she could put down her own. "I hope I wasn't interrupting anything."

"Not at all," Mac said. "We were finished. You said you were looking for me?"

She held out a wrinkled piece of paper. "I found this in the dining room just now." When Mac took it, she picked up a strawberry from her plate. "It was wadded up into a ball next to the trash can. I assume somebody missed it, so I picked it up to drop it in, and then I noticed that dollar figure." She took a small bite of the strawberry.

Mac took a quick look at the paper, and set it on the table in front of Maris. "Read it," he said, "but don't touch it." He stood up. "I'm going to the SUV and get an evidence container bag." With that, he strode off.

"But I touched it," Kaitlyn said, her eyes wide.

"There's no need to worry," Maris assured her. "The only thing that will happen is that your fingerprints will be taken."

"I hope so," the young actress said, not sounding convinced, as she put the strawberry back on the plate.

The piece of paper was stationary from Odyssey Studios, Fritz Falschung's company. It was a brief letter, dated a week from yesterday, and addressed to First Mate Lloyd Kunkel. In it, the director was offering him the captaincy, effective immediately. As

Kaitlyn had already noted, the offer letter ended in a salary figure—a rather generous one. It was signed by Fritz Falschung.

Maris narrowed her eyes at it. The director had somehow neglected to mention his plan to replace Hazelwood with his underling. It would appear that it wasn't just a matter of trying to have two directors on the same movie—one was going to fire the other.

Or had Fritz known that Hazelwood wouldn't be around much longer to pilot the ship?

The sound of Mac's quick footsteps signaled his returned. He was wearing a pair of latex gloves and was carrying a clear plastic sleeve. He picked up the offer letter and gently slipped it into the sleeve, sealing the top.

Kaitlyn watched him, sitting stock still, her eyes never leaving the letter. "Did I do something wrong?" she asked. "I'm not in trouble, am I?"

"No," Mac said. "But this is evidence in a murder investigation and you happened to have touched it." He set it back down on the table.

Then he took a small plastic box and

something that looked like an index card from his jacket pocket.

"Fingerprints," Maris said to Kaitlyn smiling. "It's just to eliminate you from the list of people who've touched it."

"Exactly," Mac said, opening the kit and putting the card at the edge of the table. "I'll start with your right-hand thumb. Just try to relax and let me do the moving."

For the next few minutes, Maris watched as Mac rolled each of the actress's fingers on a black pad, moved it to the card, and repeated the procedure, leaving her black print on it.

"I can't believe this is happening," she muttered. "I've never been fingerprinted before."

"It's standard," Mac said, his tone reassuring. When he finished, he took a moist towelette packet from the other jacket pocket and handed it to her. "Done."

Kaitlyn quickly tore it open and used it to clean her fingers, but the little towelette was already getting dark. She looked around, but only saw the linen napkins.

"Excuse me," she said. "I've got to wash this off."

As she got up and hurried off, Mac picked up the offer letter. "I think it's time to speak with Fritz."

10

Maris followed Mac down the stairs where Nadia had taken them yesterday, and nearly ran into her. Clipboard in hand, she was climbing to the deck.

"Sheriff," she said, surprised. "Maris." She smiled at the two of them as she backed down a step into the wood-paneled hallway. "I didn't know you were aboard." She looked between the two of them, and then at the evidence bag that Mac held in his gloved hands. "Is there, uh, something that I can help you with?"

"We need to speak with Fritz," Mac said, in a brisk and no-nonsense tone.

"Um, sure," Nadia said, backing up against the wall. She pointed with a pen down the hallway. "Past the fitness center, all the way at the end."

"Thank you," Mac said, heading that way, and Maris exchanged a quick look with Nadia.

Maris had to trot a little to keep up with the sheriff. They stopped outside the polished teak door, and Mac immediately knocked. He waited for a few moments, and when there was no sound from within, he knocked again. Again they waited, and Mac glanced over his shoulder at Maris who lifted her hands and shrugged.

"Maybe he's not in?" she said.

Mac pounded on the door. "Mr. Falschung," he said loudly. "It's Sheriff McKenna. Open the door."

A loud muttering came from inside, then a banging, some stomping, and two failed attempts to turn the doorknob before the door opened.

"What in the bloody hell?" the director yelled. He was wearing a very rumpled and stained white dinner jacket, and gripped the edge of the door to keep his balance. "Who in the hell do you..." He scowled at Mac's face, and then took in the uniform. "Oh," he said.

He stood up a little straighter, and leveled his bloodshot eyes at both of them. "Sheriff," he said, his voice gravelly. He shoved the door the rest of the way open. "Come in."

As they entered, he struggled to close the door behind them but it had jammed over the top of some clothes on the floor. He gave up on it with a huff, and lumbered over to the intercom next to the king-sized bed, thumbing it on.

"Coffee," he yelled, but then groaned and put a hand to his head.

"Yes, Mr. Falschung," came the monotone reply from the mesh panel, as the director put his forehead to the wall and took in a deep breath.

Although Mac was watching the director, Maris took a moment to look at their surroundings. If she had to guess, she'd say that an entire teak forest had been sacrificed for the yacht's interior. Though the director's state rooms were no more opulent than the rest of the boat, they were enormous. They'd entered into a beautifully appointed sitting area, with tasteful flower arrangements on the surrounding counters, and more of the world photography that they'd seen in the hallways. The wet bar was generously stocked, and Maris realized for the first time that every flat surface on the furniture was rimmed with a small rail, likely to prevent objects from slipping off in choppy seas.

Beyond the sitting room, built-in cabinetry flanked the round, king-sized bed, which faced a screen that could have been used in a small cinema. A dressing room beyond the bedroom held floor to ceiling closets, some open, with their drawers pulled out. Windows to the ocean on the far wall let in a beautiful light through the shear blinds.

Fritz collapsed into one of the low armchairs. "To what do I owe this inestimable, early-morning pleasure?"

Without a word, the sheriff handed him the sheet of paper in its evidence bag to him. For a few moments Fritz simply tried to focus on it. He held it at arm's length, and Maris could see his lips moving as he read it. Then he scowled.

"What is this?" he demanded. "Where did you get this?"

"Is that your company stationary?" Maris asked.

"So what if it is?" he shot back. He glared

at her and then Mac. "You didn't answer my question." When neither of them volunteered any information, Fritz tossed the bag and enclosed paper to the floor. "I didn't write that."

"Is that your signature?" Mac asked, not bothering to pick it up.

Fritz leaned forward in the chair, and then apparently thought better of it and sat back with a grunt. "You think I offered the captain's job to the first mate?" he said loudly. Then understanding seemed to dawn. "Oh, I see. This is your evidence that I knew the captain would be dead. That I was planning to replace him." He barked a sharp laugh. "Preposterous and, I might add, stupid. Anyone could get their hands on that stationary."

"*Not* anyone," Mac countered. "And it's your company."

"For your information," Fritz said, sounding as if he were speaking to a child, "I didn't like either of them. You'd think the first mate ought to be able to obey the ship's rules. No fraternization." He chopped the air in front of him. "Pure and simple. No fraternization among the crew." He glanced at the hallway. "It's a big ship, but it's still a ship. No one is going to carry on an affair here and not be seen."

At that moment, a young male steward appeared in the open doorway holding a silver service tray.

"Come, come," the director said, waving him in. "Be quick."

The steward set the silver service on the table between the three of them, and Maris noted a bottle of aspirin on it. No doubt Fritz's hungover state was not something new. Quickly the young man began to set out three cups and saucers.

"Not for them," Falschung said angrily. He took the coffee pot from him and poured a half cup for himself. "Now, get out." As the steward hurried back to the door, the director downed the entire half cup in one monstrous gulp. He watched as the young man tried to close the door. "Leave it," he bellowed, and quickly pressed a hand to his temple. As he watch the steward leave, he muttered, "Bloody useless." He was in the midst of pouring himself another half cup, when he stopped and a sly look stole over his face. He grinned at Mac. "I can't hire the first mate as captain." He sat back in his chair, holding the cup to his stomach. "Do you know why that is, Sheriff?" He took a sip.

Maris saw Mac's jaw muscles working. "I'm sure you'll enlighten me."

The director's gaze slid over to Maris. "Nadia's friend, do you know why I can't hire the first mate?"

Now it was Maris's turn to grind her teeth, but all she said was, "No."

Fritz chuckled, and smiled down into his cup. "Because he's the first mate, that's why." He looked up at them both. "He's not *licensed* to captain a ship." Then, as if for emphasis he added, "He's not legal to run a vessel like *Copernicus*. I'd void every insurance policy from here to Shanghai if I hired him."

Though Mac didn't say a word, he picked up the letter in its clear bag.

The smile on the director's face vanished. "I need some aspirin." He grabbed the bottle, flipped off the top with his thumb, and poured several into his mouth before loudly swallowing. "And a lawyer." He stared at Mac. "This conversation is over."

11

When Maris followed Mac into the hallway and up the stairs, she blew out a sigh of relief. "What an ego," she muttered. "I don't know how you put up with people like that."

To her astonishment, Mac looked behind him and gave her a smile. "By getting to the truth," he said.

As they emerged onto the sunlit deck, Maris saw that the fog had lifted, as it always did. Here in the fresh morning breeze, with the warmth of the sun on her face, she took a deep breath. Mac was right. She was here to help a friend who had called for her aid.

Maris had left people like Fritz far behind in the hospitality trade. It pained her to know what Nadia—everyone on-board—had to put up with. Yet Nadia had seemed happy with her choice, and her compensation. Likewise the first mate had seemed genuinely excited to be traveling the world.

Mac came to a stop just beyond the conversation pit and lifted the letter. "I don't think Falschung cares about licensing or any seafaring legalities. His story of worrying about insurance policies is just that."

Maris nodded. "Agreed."

He lowered the letter. "But there's no denying how fortuitous the discovery of this letter was." He glanced down at it. "I'll have it fingerprinted and the signature checked but..." He glanced outside.

"It might be time to question its discoverer," Maris finished.

As they moved to the aft deck, Mac checked along the right hand railing, while Maris sighted down the other.

"Here," Mac said, waving Maris over.

About midway down the side of the ship, in the sunlight, Kaitlyn was standing against the handrail, while the portly cinematographer used a phone to take a picture of her. As Maris and Mac approached, he handed the phone to the young actress and she smiled down at it. She looked up when she heard them approaching, and showed them the screen.

"Alan is shooting some new headshots for me," she said. "What do you think?"

Maris peered at it in the bright sunlight but could make out the young actress's winning smile. "Lovely," she said. "I can't imagine you'd take anything other than a wonderful photo."

"The camera loves her," Alan put in.

Kaitlyn swiped to the next shot, and looked up at Maris.

Pixie Point Bay glittered in the background and, in this one, Kaitlyn tilted her head a bit, her smile genuine and endearing. Though the young actress might appear waif-like in person, she looked perfectly proportioned in the photos.

"Stunning," Maris said, and Kaitlyn beamed. For a second, Maris was struck by the strangeness of the scene. A Hollywood starlet was asking her opinion on a headshot. But the amazing part was that Kaitlyn really seemed to care what she thought. "I'm sure these are going to work wonderfully for you."

"Thanks," she said, and a little color rose

into her cheeks. "Alan did a great job." She glanced at the big man. "I mean, as long as we're stuck here, and there's a cinematographer on-board, why not get something done, right?"

Alan smiled and nodded his agreement.

Mac said, "Kaitlyn, I've got a few questions for you. Would now be a good time?"

"Oh," the actress said, blinking at him. She turned off the phone. "Um, sure."

"I think I hear my cue," the cinematographer said, and turned to go.

"Thanks for your help, Alan," Kaitlyn said.

"Any time," he replied before he headed off.

Kaitlyn took a breath and squared her shoulders. "Ready."

Mac gave her a little smile. "It's not going to be as bad as all that. I won't even be using bright lights in a dark room. Promise."

Both Maris and Kaitlyn laughed, and the young actress relaxed.

The sheriff handed the evidence bag to Maris and took out his notepad. "Did you know Captain Hazelwood?"

Kaitlyn shook her head as she leaned

back against the railing. "Not at all. I mean, I don't know when the crew eats, but the captain only ate with us once or twice. He wasn't much of a talker. I think I heard that he'd been in the navy."

If Maris had to guess, the crew likely ate in the kitchen. Though the yacht was large and the guest rooms sumptuous, she had yet to see the crew quarters.

Mac made a few notes. "And how do you know Mr. Falschung?"

"I had a supporting role in *Fully Loaded*," she answered. But when she saw Mac's raised eyebrows, she added, "His last movie."

"Ah," Mac said. "That's where you met."

"Right," Kaitlyn said. "It was just a casting call, something my agent told me about. But I landed the roll of the daughter and Fritz and I hit it off. I think we really share the same vision for the work."

According to Fritz, they shared much more than that, Maris thought, and she wondered how Mac would broach that topic.

He focused on his notepad but asked. "And is that why you're here on the *Copernicus*? Because you hit it off."

Kaitlyn laughed lightly. "Oh no. I'm here to give notes on the next project."

Maris glanced at Mac. "Give notes?" she asked.

The young actress nodded quickly. "I've never really done it before, but it's so exciting."

Maris cocked her head. "Really? And why is that?"

"Hold on," Mac said, putting up his hand. "Maybe you should explain what 'giving notes' means." Maris nodded in agreement.

"Oh sorry," Kaitlyn said and rolled her eyes. "I forget that you guys aren't in the industry." She thought for a moment. "Well, it's basically making comments on the script."

"Okay," Mac said. "You're here to make comments on the script." He looked up from the notepad. "But couldn't you just do that, say, in an e-mail?"

Kaitlyn shrugged. "Sure." Then she grinned, and Maris glimpsed the little girl who'd just struck it big. "And miss out on all this." She gestured with both hands to the surroundings. "But really, giving notes is more than that. At this stage of the project, when it's not cast in concrete, you have a chance to change it."

"So the director asks for your feedback on the script," Maris said, "and then takes it to the script writer?"

Kaitlyn shook her head. "Fritz wrote the script. He's his own screenwriter. He'll take my notes, and Alan's, the producer's, the lead actors, and whoever else he trusts, and then he'll make the decision on what changes he wants. He's an absolute genius when it comes to that stuff."

"It sounds complicated," Maris said. "I always thought there was a writer who's job it was to write the whole thing."

"Sometimes," Kaitlyn said. "But it's a lot harder to write a script than it looks. I should know. I wrote one."

"You did?" Maris said. "Really?"

Kaitlyn laughed. "Every waiter and waitress in LA has written one. It doesn't mean they're any good. But I went the extra step. I hired a script doctor." At Maris's quizzical look she added, "I paid him to rewrite the whole thing."

"Wow," Maris said. "How did it turn out?"

Kaitlyn shrugged. "I liked it, but it went nowhere. It's a lot easier to give notes."

"Since you're giving notes," Maris said, "does that mean that you'll be part of the next movie?"

Kaitlyn nodded vigorously. "It's already been announced," she gushed, and clasped her hands together. "I'll be playing the love interest in this one."

Maris had to smile at the young woman's excitement.

"Can you tell me where you were at the time of the murder?" Mac asked.

"Oh," Kaitlyn said, blinking. "Right. I was in my room, thank goodness. I'd hate to have seen..." She glanced down the long deck on the side of the ship. "Well, I'm just glad I was in my room."

Maris exchanged a brief look with Mac.

"Is there anyone that can corroborate that?" the sheriff asked.

She put a finger to her chin as she thought. "Well, I didn't have any food or tea or anything brought up, and I was alone, so I guess–" She stopped and held up her finger. "Yes," she declared. "Check my social media.

I was posting some photos for my fans on the different channels."

Social media? Maris had to wonder if that was a new one for Mac—it was for her.

But he simply said, "Good," and closed the notepad. "I'll do that. Thank you for your time."

"My pleasure," she said smiling. "That wasn't so bad!"

12

As Maris watched Kaitlyn leave, nearly skipping down the deck, Mac's phone rang.

He took it from his belt. "McKenna." His slate gray eyes flicked toward the pier's parking lot. "Got it. I'm on my way."

"I've got to go," he said, as he replaced the phone in its holder. Maris handed him the evidence bag with the offer letter. "I'll let you know on this," he said, holding it up.

"Maybe we'll catch a break," Maris said, as they headed to the gangway.

"I'm not holding my breath," he said, motioning for her to go first. "And there's still another member of the crew that we should speak with."

That had to be Nadia. Maris was confident of her friend's innocence, but she might well be able to shed some light on the murder. Over time, the staff became invisible and sometimes overheard things.

"Right," Maris said as they reached the bottom.

He paused as she caught up. "Are you headed to the parking lot?"

"Not right away," she said. "I'm going to check on Slick."

"All right," the sheriff said, hesitating for a moment, as though he was unsure of which direction to go. Abruptly, he said, "I'll be in touch."

"Great," Maris said, smiling. "I'm looking forward to it."

Though he looked like he might have a reply, he only smiled and strode in the direction of the lot.

Maris went the short distance to where Slick's boat was docked. When she didn't see him on the deck, she passed the pointed prow and caught the faintest hint of...turpentine. Down below, there was Slick in the shadow of the wheelhouse, painting.

"Ahoy, there," she called down to him. "Permission to come aboard?"

Slick looked up and smiled, waving the paintbrush. "Always granted."

Maris hurried to the gangway and down it, and met Slick at the wood platform that separated *Seas the Day* from *Copernicus*. He held out his hand to her, which she gratefully accepted, and helped her down into the boat.

"Two visits in one day," he said. "I'll have to stay in port more often."

Maris gave him a quick hug. "That would suit me fine," she said. As they separated she eyed the paintbrush. "You can't stop working, can you."

He gave her a measured raise of one bushy eyebrow. "Look who's talking."

Maris had taken after her Aunt Glenda in many respects, from her looks to her magic ability and even her adopted cat. But Slick was referring to the Type A+ personality that she and Glenda had shared.

"Show me what you're doing," she said.

He took her hand to keep her steady on the deck, and they circled to the other side of the wheelhouse. Then he guided her to a wooden crate, where she took a seat. A piece of paint spattered canvas covered the deck next to the small building that housed the boat's controls. As Slick stepped back onto it, he dipped the brush into an open paint can.

"Too early in the season for painting," he said, as if to himself. "But flogging the glass is permitted if you can't sail." He was painting the trim on the white wheelhouse a beautiful, royal blue.

"That's a wonderful color," Maris said.

He stopped for a moment and admired it. "The color of a deep and becalmed sea, just before a winter storm."

In her mind's eye, Maris saw it—the water like a glassy jewel under the gray skies.

He dipped his brush again. "Making headway up there?" he asked.

"Yes," Maris said, glad to be able to tell the truth. "I think we're narrowing in on it." Even so, she was glad when he didn't press her for a timeline. As Mac had said, they still needed to talk with Nadia. But thinking of questioning her former colleague, made something else occur to her. They had yet to question Slick. "When Hazelwood fell dead on the deck, wouldn't you have heard him?"

Slick kept painting. "I wasn't here," he said. "I'd been in the processing warehouse, at the end of the pier, sorting out the day's catch. Then I'd gone home." He dunked the brush again. "I saw the flare gun when I came back aboard this morning." He paused to look at her. "The rest you know."

"Was anyone else in the warehouse that evening?" she asked. Although she knew that Slick was innocent, she preferred the question come from her, and not Mac.

"Nope," he said simply, painting again. "Too late for the landlubbers."

Maris had to smile a little at his seeming...quiet confidence? Nonchalance? Lack of concern? The only thing that seemed to ruffle the old sailor was not sailing. She'd been about to remark on that fact, when she heard voices.

Slick stopped painting. He'd heard them too, and they were growing louder.

She looked toward the front of *Seas the Day*. Judging from the direction of the voices, whoever was speaking must have been on the prow of the *Copernicus*, only several feet away. Though she couldn't see them because of the wheelhouse, they sounded so close now they couldn't be on the pier.

"Leave it to Captain Bligh to get murdered before we could push him overboard," a baritone said.

Maris grimaced a little at the reference. The sailors aboard the *HMS Bounty* had mutinied and cast their hated captain adrift with his supporters.

"Too bad that someone beat us to it," the other, higher-pitched, voice said.

"Too bad they were so stupid," the baritone said. "Now there's a murder investigation."

"Quit your griping," the other protested. "We're in the clear."

There was a pause. Maris tried to imagine the speakers, as far forward on the yacht as they could be, and thinking that they couldn't be overheard.

"It would have been cleaner our way," the baritone said. "We'd have said 'bad weather' and been done with it, *and* still sailing."

"True," the higher-pitched voice agreed. "The sooner Lloyd takes over and we get underway, the better."

"I hear it's Captain Lloyd now," the baritone said.

"When?" said the other.

"He says three months back. Course complete, sea experience documented, licensed, everything."

Maris's eyebrows flew up, and Slick simply nodded.

"Here comes Kaitlyn," the baritone said, barely audible. Then in a louder voice, "Ms. Cameron. Stretching your legs?"

"I thought I'd walk the pier," she said, and the voices drifted off.

13

———

When Maris arrived home at the B&B, she found the parking slots empty, except for Bear's truck. Their mountain-of-a-man handyman was here nearly as much as they were. The Victorian home and lighthouse were in constant need of upkeep and repair—and the young man was pleasant to have around.

Inside the B&B, Maris went to her room and was about to toss her purse on the bed, but found Mojo sprawled there and napping. Instead she put her purse on the dressing table, and gave him a gentle belly rub. Though he stretched his legs and toes a little, he made no move to get up.

"Smart cat," she whispered.

Quietly, she left the room, thinking about

the conversation that she and Slick had overheard. Before she'd begun looking into local crimes, Maris would have called Mac with the information immediately. But now, she hesitated.

"Hearsay at best," she muttered as she wandered toward the public rooms. She hadn't seen who was talking and, even if she had, it was little more than gossip. Could she even be sure they'd been serious?

From the back porch vestibule, Maris could see Cookie in her herb garden, as she usually was in the afternoon, and Bear trailing behind her with two big bags of fertilizer.

"Hey, you two," Maris said, as she came down the porch's few steps.

"Hello, Maris," Bear said, his brown eyes smiling over his full mustache and beard.

Despite the fact that each of the manure bags had to weigh as much as Cookie, he simply held them against his burgeoning middle as though they were pillows.

"Maris," Cookie said, using the back of a gloved hand to brush a lock of hair out of her eyes. "What's happening at the pier?"

"Well, we've spoken to just about

everyone on the yacht," she said, "and the list of suspects is narrowing."

Cookie picked up a small trowel from a bucket near her feet. "But no arrests," she said.

Maris shook her head. "I'm afraid not."

"Is Slick okay?" Bear asked, his brow furrowing.

Like Cookie and herself, Bear was one of the magic folk. But unlike most of the other residents of Pixie Point Bay, Maris knew his ability. He was a shifter—a kind-hearted, un-complicated, and bee-keeping shifter.

"Yes," Maris told him. "I think he is. Of course, he'd rather be out fishing, but I saw him twice today and he's making good use of his time, mending nets and painting the boat."

Cookie was using the trowel to dig a small hole next to one of the plants. "Another couple days of this and we'll be running out of fresh salmon."

Bear's eyes widened and he stared at her. "Run out?" The big man cast a worried look to Maris, then back to Cookie, and then at the bay.

"You can set those there, Bear," she said,

indicating the border of the large herb garden. "And yes, run out."

The diminutive chef had said this from the start, and Maris hadn't believed it. But after seeing the fisherman at the pier this morning and talking with Ryan, she had to wonder.

Bear set down the bags and Cookie opened one with her trowel, scooping out the rich compost and shoveling it in the small hole. "What's it like being with the rich and famous?" she asked.

Maris thought of Kaitlyn and then of Fritz and Alan. "I suppose they're like regular folks, really. Some nice and some not so nice." Then she recalled the ship and the way it dwarfed Slick's boat. "It's like a little floating world, that yacht. Just incredible." She shared some of the more extravagant details. "Honestly, I've never seen lavish accommodations like it, not even in my hospitality career."

Cookie finished digging another hole and Bear brought the compost cupped in his two big hands.

"Makes Pixie Point Bay look a little backwards by comparison," Cookie said.

Bear dumped in the fertilizer and dusted off his hands.

"Backwards?" Maris said, looking at the two-story house. "I'd say comfortable, warm, and inviting. The *Copernicus* is shiny and sleek, but it's not a home."

Hands on hips, Cookie smiled at her. "I stand corrected."

"Speaking of home," Maris said, glancing at the house, "I think I'd better see to some chores while the guests are out."

Inside, with just the one couple staying with them, the duties were light. Maris made the bed and took out the trash. Cookie had already seen to her share, providing them with fresh towels and cleaning the bathroom. Maris also checked the public rooms, dusting a little and straightening up, before gathering up more trash.

The more she mulled over the conversation she'd overheard, the more she decided to call Mac and tell him. Although she wouldn't exactly call it evidence, it would be up to him what he wanted to do with it.

She'd been headed to the trash bins outside when the landline rang. She picked up the antique handset.

"Pixie Point Bay Lighthouse and B&B," she said pleasantly. "How can I help you?"

"Maris," said that familiar voice again. "It's Slick."

She set down the trash bag. "What's wrong?" She heard a siren in the background. "Slick, are you okay?"

"I think you'd better get back here," he said. "Someone on the *Copernicus* has died."

14

By the time Maris parked at the pier, it was a scene of déjà vu. The stretcher, with a black body bag, was being loaded into the coroner's van. Maris hurried down the dock to Slick's boat. Impossibly, she found him still painting.

"Slick," she called down to him, a little breathless. "Are you all right?"

"Aı," he said smiling, and set down the brush. "You must have had the wind in your sails."

"Who died?" she asked. "Do you know?"

He shook his head. "Nope." He shrugged. "It didn't happen on my boat."

Her mind immediately went to Nadia and Kaitlyn, and she prayed that they were okay.

As she turned to head to the yacht, she

looked up at its deck. Several people were standing at the railing. Nadia was there, and Kaitlyn too, and Maris put a hand to her heart and exhaled. Then she took a head count. Five people wore the white uniforms of the crew, including Nadia and Lloyd. That meant they were all accounted for. Alan was at the railing, next to Kaitlyn, so that only left...

"Fritz?" she said, and then spotted Mac at the bottom of the gangway. He waved her over. Quickly, she made her way down the pier to the walkway. "Fritz Falschung is dead?"

The sheriff raised an eyebrow at her. "Slick told you?"

"No," she said glancing up at the railing. "I did a quick head count. He was the only one missing. Unless there was a stranger on the boat?"

"No, you're right," he said. "Falschung is dead."

Her stomach sank and she put both hands to her cheeks. They'd only been speaking with him—arguing with him— hours ago. And now he was dead?

"Are you all right?" Mac said quietly.

Lowering her hands, she nodded. "It's just that...." She shook her head. "How did he die?"

Despite an obvious hangover after a night of partying, he'd seemed fit.

"The Turkish sauna," Mac said. "He was inside and couldn't get out."

Maris cocked her head back. "Good grief." Instantly she pictured him when they'd first met, coming from the sauna in his captain's hat and purple robe.

"We'll have to wait for the coroner's report," Mac said, glancing in the direction of the van. "It could be that alcohol or some other substance might have been involved. Something that would have impeded his judgement." The sheriff looked back at her. "But I don't think that's it."

His calm manner told her he knew more. "What did you find?" she asked, almost not wanting to hear the answer.

"The doorknob," he said. "It was lying on the floor inside. When he needed to get out he couldn't."

"The doorknob?" she said, incredulous. "Just lying on the floor? It fell off?"

Mac shook his head. "I've got it in the

SUV, so the lab has yet to see it. But the knob, like most doorknobs, was only held on with a set screw. I found that on the floor too."

Maris tried to imagine it, and cocked her head. "So the screw came loose? You're saying it was an accident."

Again Mac shook his head. "The screw head was stripped—worn down. Even on the off chance that Falschung had possessed a hex screwdriver and had it on his person in the sauna and tried to reattach the knob, it wouldn't have worked." He paused for a moment as Maris nodded. "The wear and tear on the hex screw looked new—shiny."

Maris's eyes widened. "You think it was deliberate. That someone wanted him trapped in the sauna."

Mac nodded. "I'd stake my career on it. It was murder."

"Two murders," Maris whispered, as she and Mac looked up to the yacht's handrail and the collection of people there. One of them had to be the murderer.

The sheriff withdrew an envelope from his jacket. "I've got a search warrant. The forensics team is on-board and has already been over the sauna and fitness rooms. We'll start in the director's room."

But as he started up the gangway, Maris put a hand on his arm and stopped him. "I was just about to call you when Slick called me. Before leaving the pier this morning I stopped at his boat to check in on him. While I was there we overheard a couple members of the crew."

"Oh?" Mac said, turning to her.

She related the brief discussion and finished with, "Unfortunately, we didn't see anyone before the conversation was interrupted."

Mac cast a sidelong glance at the yacht's guests and crew. "Captain Bligh," he said quietly. "Maybe Falschung had been telling the truth about the captain being hated."

How that helped them with this second murder, Maris didn't know. But then a thought occurred to her. "Could Fritz have known who the murderer was and not told us? He might have confronted the person himself."

"I wouldn't put it past him," the sheriff said. "Either way, two murders on one yacht is not a coincidence. Let's start our search."

15

———

As Maris and Mac joined the crew and guests on the deck, there was a grim, stunned silence. But to no one's surprise, Lloyd stepped forward.

"Sheriff, Maris," he said. "Some of the crew and staff need to get back to their duties. Would that be all right?"

"Honestly," Mac said. "No. If you'll give me and the forensics team a couple of hours for a search, I'd rather you all wait here."

The guests and crew looked at one another, but no one objected. Nadia gave Maris a questioning look, but Maris could only raise her hands and shrug.

"We run the risk of losing evidence," Mac said.

Lloyd surveyed the crew and guests and said, "I think we can do that."

"Thanks," Mac said, "I appreciate it."

Although the sheriff had turned away, Lloyd hurried forward, and lowered his voice. "I performed an inventory of our emergency gear," he said. "We have a dry storage box on the skiff, and...it was missing its flare gun and a cartridge."

Mac regarded him. "I take it no one has used it of late, in an emergency?"

The first mate frowned and shook his head. "Not since I've been aboard."

"All right," Mac said, "thank you." Silently, he led the way back to the stairs, and then glanced over his shoulder. "No surprise there," he said. "But I'm glad he came forward with the information."

"Me too," Maris said with some relief. Though she'd always known that Slick could not be involved, it was good to have evidence on his side too.

As they made their way to Fritz's room, Maris couldn't help but be struck again by a sense of déjà vu. The door was still ajar, though the clothes seemed to have been moved. Mac paused at the threshold, dug in his pants pocket, and offered a pair of blue latex gloves to Maris.

"They haven't dusted for fingerprints yet," he said, and then he put on his pair.

"Thanks," Maris said, and put on hers.

Mac went directly to the bathroom and the medicine cabinet, so Maris headed to the desk. On it she found Fritz's tablet. She pressed the home button, and the screen blazed to life. Apparently the director didn't believe in password protection. She swiped past dozens of applications, until she'd gone through several screens, and then went back to the home page. The voice memo app caught her attention. They'd seen him use it only yesterday.

Mac brought an armload of pill bottles from the bathroom and put them on the wet bar, with the ample supply of liquor.

Maris touched the voice memo icon and it started up. At the top of a list of time-stamped recordings, were two from yesterday. Recognizing the time when they'd inter-viewed him, she touched that link first.

In an eerie moment that made Mac look up from his search of the nightstands, Fritz's voice came from the machine. Maris turned up the volume. They heard him opine on what it was like being a suspect in a murder case.

"How ironic," Maris said, when it finished. She touched the next link.

In this brief recording, he sketched out some ideas for characters in his noir movie. "The cop has to be plodding, not exactly the village idiot, but close. He's accompanied by a nosy local hotel owner who likes to pry into everyone's business, so of course, she's not well liked."

Maris raised an eyebrow as the recording finished. "Nosy," she muttered.

"Better than 'village idiot'," Mac said, smirking.

He scooped out some blister packs of pills from the nightstand drawers and put them with the others. "There's enough here for a pharmacy," he said, surveying it all. "Amphetamines, sedatives, a psychedelic or two, even some pot."

But Maris didn't look up at the assembled drugs, she'd found a folder labeled "Fully Loaded".

"Wasn't 'Fully Loaded' the name of his

last movie?" Maris asked. "The one that Kaitlyn told us about?"

Mac had gone over to the closets. "Yes," he said. "That was it. For a moment, I didn't realize it was a movie."

Maris clicked on that folder and it opened up to reveal several documents. She clicked on "Fully Loaded Final 2".

Though Maris had never read a script before, that was clearly what she was seeing: character names for each bit of dialogue, sparse instructions for the camera, and brief descriptions of the settings. But as she scrolled down, the text began to change color. In the beginning, it had all been black, and in a font that looked like an old typewriter had created it.

But now it was a mix of black text and blue text, though Maris couldn't see any pattern to it. About midway through the document, the text was a mishmash of black, blue, and now red colors. Finally, it became entirely red. As Maris scrolled up and down, she recalled Kaitlyn's explanation of giving notes. Is that what she was seeing? Whoever had been writing with the red text had done the lion's share of the work, but the document looked like an unmitigated mess. How anyone could have made a movie from it was beyond her.

Raised voices came from down the hallway, causing Maris and Mac to both stop their searches.

Maris set the tablet down and followed Mac outside to find the narrow hallway jammed. Nadia and Kaitlyn were both pulling suitcases behind them, while Lloyd appeared to be trying to clear a way for them.

"What's going on here?" Mac said loudly over the cacophony of voices. When no one heard him, he put his fingers to his lips and gave a short loud whistle. Everyone stopped and turned to him. "What's going on here?"

"I'm not staying one more minute on this ship," Kaitlyn declared. "I've had it."

There was grumbling from the crew who'd gathered on the stairs, and Maris couldn't tell if they were leaving as well, or angry that the others were fleeing.

"Pipe down," Lloyd ordered, silencing the men. He turned to Mac. "Sheriff, this was my idea, and I accept full responsibility."

"All right, Lloyd," Mac said, sounding the

voice of reason. "Why don't you tell me what this is about?"

"We've had two murders in as many days," the first mate said. "I was talking to Kaitlyn, upside where we were waiting–"

"And I decided I don't want to be murdered," she finished for him.

Mac made a motion for her to slow down. "I'm not going to force you to stay," he said, reassuringly. "No one has to stay on this ship." The assembled group all looked at one another, and the tension dropped about three notches.

"Thank you, Sheriff," Lloyd said. "I'll be staying aboard, but I'm insisting that Kaitlyn and Ms. Malakin leave."

"If the crew is staying," Nadia interjected. "Then I'm staying."

Another round of interchanges took place. "Nadia, please," Lloyd said.

"Do what you want," Kaitlyn said.

"Just set sail," said someone from the stairs.

Mac whistled, bringing silence again. Not for the first time, Maris wished she knew how to do that.

"If you leave the vessel," Mac said, "then I

must ask you to stay close by." He looked at Lloyd. "Nor can the ship leave port. It's a crime scene. But I am not forcing anyone to stay on board. That's up to you."

"Ms. Malakin and Kaitlyn are leaving," Lloyd said. "I'm staying with the ship." He glanced behind him to where the other crew members had gathered, all of them men. "Anyone else?" For a few awkward moments there was only the shuffling of feet and downward glances. "Well?" the first mate asked. He waited for a few seconds. "Then let's get back on deck and wait as we were instructed." He picked up both Kaitlyn and Nadia's suitcases and started up the stairs.

"Maybe you should arrest us," Kaitlyn said glumly. "Then at least we'd have a place to stay."

Maris held up her hand, looking pointedly at Kaitlyn and then at Nadia. "I have the perfect place," she said.

16

As Maris turned down the bed, Kaitlyn set her suitcase on the wood and embroidered linen luggage rack.

"What a lovely room," the young actress said, turning around to take it in. "The yacht is nice, but I forgot how small the rooms are." She went to the rose-colored, sheer, lace curtains at the window and held them aside. "Wow," she whispered. "Look at that."

Maris smiled to herself as she turned on the oil radiator. That particular window looked up the coast, to the north and the pier. The setting sun had begun to bathe the bay in rich amber tones, turning the water into a mirror made of hammered and polished copper.

Once the heater had started to warm, Maris opened the armoire next to the full length dressing mirror. A soft, white terrycloth robe hung on one of the many padded satin hangers, and new slippers lay in the bottom. Everything was ready.

"Please do take your time settling in," Maris said, turning to her. "The bathroom is just outside to your left and you'll be sharing with Nadia. We'll have wine and cheese in the dining room shortly. If there's anything else you need, please just let me know."

Kaitlyn turned from the window, her eyes a bit misty. "Thank you, Maris. You can't imagine how much I appreciate this."

Maris inclined her head as she closed the door. "It's entirely my pleasure."

As she crossed the short hallway, she peeked in the bathroom, even though she'd already seen that it was stocked with clean towels and toiletries. The door to Nadia's room was open. Maris knocked lightly at the threshold.

Nadia's suitcase was already open but she was sitting on the taupe settee. Her back was to the south facing window, with its view of the setting sun through the open shutters.

Her shoulders hunched and there were dark circles under her eyes. It was a look that Maris knew well.

"May I turn down the bed?" Maris asked.

Nadia smiled weakly. "The last thing I want to do is create more work for you."

Maris smiled and took that as an invitation to enter. "You're doing nothing of the sort," she said, turning down the linen sheets and comforter, and arranging the pillows. "We're not even close to being at full capacity."

Nadia glanced around at the Victorian furnishings, the Tiffany lamps, and the dusty blue of the ceiling and its decorative medallions. "I don't know how you can't be overbooked," she said. "Your B&B is absolutely stunning."

Maris turned on the oil radiator, and opened the armoire. "High praise indeed," she said, grinning at her former colleague. "But we don't overbook. If there's a cancellation, then there's a cancellation." She took a pair of uniform pants from the suitcase and hung them, then the accompanying shirt.

"You don't need to do that," Nadia said, but seemed rooted to the settee.

"I know," Maris said simply, hanging up another blouse. "It just gives me a minute to tell you that the bathroom is just outside to the right, and you'll be sharing it with Kaitlyn."

Nadia finally turned to look at the view south. The rocky coastline undulated into the distance, and the sun had begun its final, fiery dip to the horizon. Maris heard her sigh.

"Take your time settling in," Maris said quietly, "and please let me know if there is anything I can do to make your stay more comfortable. The Wine Down starts in just a bit."

Nadia turned back to her. "A Wine Down?" It was the affectionate term that those in the industry used for the evening wine and cheese. "Oh that sounds wonderful." Maris smiled back at her and began to close the door. "Maris?" Nadia said, stopping her. "This is exactly what I needed. Thank you."

"You know I'm speaking the truth," Maris told her, "when I say it's absolutely my pleasure." With that, she left Nadia in her room.

Downstairs, Maris went straight to the Muenster in the fridge, doubly glad now that she'd stocked up in Cheeseman Village. She'd already decided it would go beautifully with the local Chenin Blanc. But for the rest of the artisanal cheeses and their pairings, she gently tapped her temple to bring up an image of the wine cabinet in the dining room and the refrigerator in the pantry. Never one to slavishly follow wine and cheese pairing dogma, she liked to let her imagination run. Slowly she made her decisions. The semi-soft provolone would pair nicely with a light California Chianti, while the sharp, aged cheddar would stand up well to the Argentinian Malbec.

With that settled, she also piled the savory crackers, some fresh figs, and nuts on the board and took it to the dining room. It was a reception technique that she'd stumbled on years ago. Rather than prepare everything in the kitchen, she found that guests liked to watch her assemble the board. It encouraged a bit of nibbling as well as conversation.

She brought in the chilled Chenin Blanc and opened it but when she reached into the bottom storage of the wine cabinet, she touched something furry that squeaked.

With a bit of a squeak herself, she jumped backward. But when she peered inside, she saw a cat toy.

"Mojo," she muttered, bringing it out. It was a furry gray mouse—another of his toys that she had yet to see. Where he kept his stash, she didn't know. But for the time being, she put the mouse back.

After bringing out the Chianti and Malbec, she opened them all and set them next to the ready glasses. The cheeses were sliced and arranged by the time Nadia and Kaitlyn arrived. Maris turned to smile at them. Both had changed and were looking decidedly more relaxed.

"I was just telling Kaitlyn," Nadia said, "how impressive your establishment here is. Truly, I am in awe of the attention to detail and the real comfort that you offer."

"Ditto," Kaitlyn said, smiling. She went to the wines and turned them to read the labels. "Help yourself?" she asked, over her shoulder.

"Please do," Maris said, then turned to Nadia. "And thank you."

They poured themselves some wine and admired the sunset out the bay window.

"What a locale," Nadia said, with something like awe in her voice.

"And an old lighthouse," Kaitlyn said, looking up at the circling beam.

"They go hand in hand," Maris said, as she finished the lavish and large cheeseboard. "The lighthouse needs to be seen throughout the bay, so we're out here on this rocky promontory."

"Ah," Nadia said, turning back to her. "That in turn gives the B&B its amazing views." Then she saw the cheeseboard. "What have we here?"

The two younger women took plates and helped themselves as Maris poured herself a glass of the Chianti.

"I love pistachios," Kaitlyn crowed. "But I'd never have thought to have them with white wine."

"Is that chutney?" Nadia said, picking up the serving spoon. "Oh goodness, that is brilliant." She heaped some on her plate with the two types of savory crackers, and a couple slices of fig. "I'm going to have to steal these ideas, you know." She gave Maris a wink.

Maris lifted her glass to them. "To the Wine Down."

"To the Wine Down," they echoed, clinking glasses.

"Looks like the party started without us," Mark Magnuson said, as he and his wife came to the dining room entrance.

Maris laughed as she turned to them. "It's not a party without the Magnusons," she said.

She made the introductions all around, and the Magnusons obviously recognized Kaitlyn.

"We loved *Fully Loaded*!" Gayle said, shaking her hand. "You were wonderful."

"Thank you," Kaitlyn said, her smile adorable.

Mark and Gayle served themselves and asked a million questions about Hollywood and the yacht, that Kaitlyn and Nadia were happy to answer. No, it never got old being recognized. Yes, it was wonderful sailing around the globe. No, it wasn't always easy remembering lines. Yes, the crew on a boat was a family.

For their part, the Magnusons heartily recommended the redwood hikes and had also spent the day using the B&B's kayaks. Though they'd never done any kayaking before, they'd found them easy to use. They'd even managed to spot otters in the bay.

"Look at that sunset," Mark said. The sky had become a vivid violet, and only the tip of the sun's orb showed.

Gayle took his arm. "Shall we go outside?" She glanced at Kaitlyn and Nadia. "All of us?"

Maris was following the amiable group to the back porch door when a tiny, tinny harmonica-like meow drew her attention to the floor. Mojo stood in the hallway, his big orange eyes watching her. But when she beckoned to him, he only meowed again, and trotted into the parlor.

"Hmm," Maris said. She knew better than to question his summons.

17

Glass of Chianti in hand, Maris followed her pudgy, little black cat into the parlor. She watched as he lightly jumped to the top of the back of the embroidered chair, and then to the bookshelf. He went directly to the box of tarot cards and began to paw it, batting it this way and that. But rather than see him knock them to the floor—where they'd likely scatter for her to pick up—she snatched the box just as it was tipping from the shelf.

Mojo mewed plaintively.

"Don't worry," she said, and set down her wine. "You'll have your chance."

She sat down on the Persian rug, removed the cards and explanation booklet from the box, and then looked up at him. "Well, come on. This was your idea."

With a couple of little leaps, he was on the floor in front of her. He cocked his head in fascination as she shuffled the deck.

"We'll do a three card spread," she told him. "You pick them."

With a sweeping motion of her hand, she fanned out the cards face down on the rug between them. He meowed again, then stepped across the cards to her lap, and nestled down. But as he'd crossed them, Maris took note of the three that he touched. She picked up the first one.

"Card one is the past," she told him, flipped it over and set it down. "Ooh, The Tower."

True to its name, this card from the major arcana featured a large dark tower. But it was burning and people were falling from it. Maris stared at the image. Captain Hazelwood had likely fallen from the yacht to the deck of Slick's boat. Fritz Falschung had essentially died from too much heat. Did this symbolize either or maybe even both of their deaths?

In her lap, eyes closed, Mojo purred.

She turned over the second. "The present," she told him. It was the Queen of Wands. At her royal feet sat a black cat. Maris had to smirk. "If that's supposed to be me, I'm missing the crown."

She revealed the final card. "The future." This card, however, was upside down, also known as the reversed position. It was the High Priestess. A woman sat in front of a thin veil, flanked by two pillars. In her lap, she held a scroll that was partly covered by her robe.

Rather than look at the little booklet of explanations, Maris lightly tapped her temple and brought up its image in memory. The reversed High Priestess directed your attention inward so that you could listen to your own voice and wisdom.

Maris glanced down at Mojo. "Is that what I'm supposed to do?"

In answer, he gave his signature meow, got up from her lap, and lightly trotted out of the room.

Great. What was that supposed to mean? "Thanks," she called out after him.

18

The next morning, Maris woke up to a late night text from Mac. He was going to be back at the yacht for more searches in the morning. She checked the time. Luckily she'd woken a little earlier than normal, but with more guests she'd need more time. She'd already planned to get up before daybreak to get to the clean laundry that was waiting in the utility room.

Quickly she showered and, hair still damp, hurried to the kitchen. Cookie was at the stove, as usual. "Everything good here? I wanted to fold the linens and sheets before I left."

Cookie turned with a smile. "Good morning. Everything here is fine. How did you sleep?"

Maris had already turned to go but stopped. "Good morning," she said quickly and smiled. She held up a finger. "Be right back."

In the laundry room, she attacked the rumpled cloth with her usual systematic fervor. First came the largest pieces, the sheets for the queen beds, then the full sheets, and pillow cases. She snapped the fabric out smartly, making sure that everything was folded to within a millimeter of its life, perfectly square and crumple free. Then came the towels, also in order of descending size, tri-folded lengthwise and then in half so that they hung wrinkle-free. She stacked all of these in the linen closet, breathing a little hard. But as she moved the newer linens to the end of the line, and the older to the front, she saw a set of sheets that had doubled over on itself.

"Rats," she said. She took these back to the laundry room, shook them out, and folded them again.

With those out of the way, she hustled back to the kitchen. But when she arrived, the warming trays had already been moved to the dining room and Cookie was lighting the burners.

"Just in time," the diminutive chef said.

"Time?" Maris asked. "It looks like you're done. I'm sorry I didn't help."

Cookie frowned at her. "Of course you helped. Just not in the kitchen."

Confused, Maris looked at the trays, the waiting plates, the juice, coffee, and hot water dispenser. "Then what am I in time for?"

"Breakfast, of course," Cookie said.

"Oh, Cookie," Maris said, "I'm afraid I don't have time. I've got to find my travel mug and–"

"Where's the fire?" Cookie asked, serving herself some oatmeal.

Maris blinked at her. "Fire?" She glanced around. Was it a play on words?

Cookie picked up a spoon. "As in, why are you in such a hurry?"

"*Oh*," Maris said exhaling and feeling a bit silly. "I've got to meet Mac at the pier."

"Okay," Cookie said taking a seat. "Does he expect you to go without breakfast? Are you late for a certain appointment?"

Though Maris grimaced a bit, she answered both questions truthfully: "No and no."

"Huh," Cookie said, as if to herself. "Imagine that. Rushing off without eating, and no particular deadline."

Maris knew very well what the B&B's chef was doing. Maris and her Aunt Glenda had both been self-acknowledged Type A personalities. But also like her aunt, she battled with her weight and cholesterol. Glenda and Maris's mother had died of heart attacks, and her mother had been younger than she was now.

"You've come here to settle down, haven't you?" Cookie said, putting her oatmeal on the table.

"Of course," Maris answered, resigning herself to defeat.

"Then settle down, young lady." Cookie eyed her and pointed to the buffet. "Settle down and eat."

Although Maris had thought to grab a piece of toast and hit the road, she opted for what the chef was having. But instead of the butter and brown sugar in her oatmeal, she decided that her battle with cholesterol would have more success with a few dried raisins and cranberries.

Cookie brought a teapot to the table and two cups, noting the time on her watch.

"I see we have two new guests as of yesterday," she said, sitting down as Maris did. "Did the yacht sink?"

Maris laughed. "No, I'm afraid not." Then she sobered as she remembered the coroner's van. "The director, Fritz Falschung, the owner of the ship, died in the sauna."

"In the sauna?" Cookie asked, staring at her.

Maris recounted the entire ordeal and all of the clues to date. Cookie poured some tea for them, and Maris finished with how both Kaitlyn and Nadia had wanted nothing more to do with the yacht after the second death.

"I can't blame them," Cookie said nodding, sipping her tea and than having some oatmeal. "Next thing you know, it'll fly the Jolly Roger and have ghosts at the wheel."

Maris had to laugh. "It certainly feels cursed," she agreed.

They chatted about Slick, and also Mojo's turns at the Ouija board and tarot cards.

Cookie wagged a finger at her. "He's listening to the spirits, that little devil. I'd stake my prize herbs on it."

Suddenly, Maris found herself having the last of her tea, and looking down at an empty bowl of oatmeal.

"That was delicious, Cookie," she said. "Thank you."

"You're very welcome, my dear," she said as Maris got up. The chef checked her watch. "How much time do you think we spent having breakfast?"

The question came out of the blue. Once Maris had decided she was not going to win any argument on slowing down for the sake of her health, she hadn't looked at her watch. She started to bring her wrist up.

"Don't look," Cookie said quickly. Maris stopped in mid-motion. "Just a guesstimate. Tell me how much time you think that you spent having breakfast."

Maris pursed her lips and tried to cheat by looking out the bay window. Unfortunately, the fog was no help. "Maybe...forty-five minutes?"

Cookie smiled and shook her head. "Twenty-five."

"No way," Maris muttered and looked at

her watch. "Or yes way." She scowled at it. Maybe it was running slow.

As if the chef had heard her thoughts, she said, "Time isn't running slow, you're running fast."

Maris had to laugh at herself. "It felt like forty-five."

Cookie stood and picked up her bowl and Maris's. "I know it did, my young friend. Slow it down. You have all the time in the world, and I want to make sure it stays that way."

As the chef passed, Maris touched her shoulder. "Thank you, Cookie."

She went back to her room, where Mojo was just rousing, took her purse, and headed to the front door. Not one of the guests had yet come down. There had indeed been plenty of time.

As she opened the door, she heard Cookie call from the kitchen. "Get Slick on the ocean. We're down to our last fresh lox."

19

———

Just as Maris was pulling into the pier's foggy parking lot, Mac was getting out of his SUV. After all of the rush and hurry, and then having to slow down for breakfast, she'd arrived on time. But Cookie was right. There was no 'on time', not really. What if the sheriff had started the search on his own? What if she'd joined him an hour from now?

But even as she thought about being late —or worse, disappointing someone—she inwardly cringed. It wasn't part of her makeup, while being in a hurry, not to mention being competitive, was. She knew the chef was trying to help and that she needed to change, but the question remained whether or not that was even possible—for anybody.

When she parked next to the sheriff's SUV and turned off the engine, Mac opened her door for her. "Good morning," he said. "You're as dependable as day following night."

"Or the morning fog," she said getting out. "And good morning to you too." He closed the door and she locked it. Their footsteps quietly thudded along the wood planks.

"So Maris," Mac began, "are you a native of Pixie Point Bay?"

"You could say that," she said. "Via Dubai, Cancun, Jackson Hole, Cairo, Singapore, and Hong Kong, just to name a few of my waypoints." Mac gave a low whistle. "But yes, Pixie Point Bay is my home. I spent a number of years here with my aunt."

Mostly it had been summers and holidays between school semesters, after her mother had died of a heart attack when Maris had been a high school senior. But from the first moment she'd stayed with Aunt Glenda at the B&B, it'd felt like home.

"That's quite the itinerary," Mac said, as they made their way up the pier. There were only a few fisherman with their lines over the railing, none of whom Maris recognized. "It has to be a huge change of pace from places like those."

"Happily," Maris said, "you're right." She gave him a sideways glance. "And where do you hail from, Mac?"

"Originally?" he asked, and Maris nodded. "A little town up north called Pine Ridge. Then police departments in Portland, Palm Springs, and Los Angeles."

"The megalopolis," she said, as they passed Slick's boat. As usual he was on deck but this time the cowling over the engine was open. Mac nodded as they passed and she waved. "Now *that* has to be a change of pace."

"A good one," he agreed. He looked out into the white mist and Maris wondered what he was seeing. "It's strange because as the Medio County sheriff my territory is probably about twenty times bigger than anything I've covered in the city." Then he looked back to her. "But it doesn't feel like that. It feels small and hometown."

Maris smiled in reply. They shared more than crime solving, which pleased her.

As they reached the gangway, Mac stood back and let her go up first. When they reached the deck, she said, "Where are we starting?"

"I finished the crew rooms yesterday," he said, "since they're still living here and needed to have access to them. Same with the cinematographer's." They took their now usual path to the back of the boat. "Nothing unusual turned up."

"So that leaves the other guest rooms?" she asked.

"Right," he said. "But after what you overheard from Slick's boat, I think we'll start with the first mate."

But when they reached the sunken conversation pit, they discovered Alan Hecht having breakfast. He saw them just as they stepped down, and smiled. "We've got to stop meeting like this."

"Good morning," Maris said.

"Mr. Hecht," the sheriff said. "Looks like you've pretty much got the boat to yourself."

The big man shrugged. "Well, it sure has been quiet." Then he cast his glance to the floor. "Especially without Fritz." Maris recalled their long history together. "I still can't believe it."

He had echoed the same words as Lloyd

about the captain. It seemed that both sides of the ship—the crew and the guests—had lost a leader.

"Find any clues?" the cinematographer asked, looking hopeful.

"Not at this point," Mac said.

"Are you enjoying your breakfast?" Maris asked. Today's fare seemed quite a bit simpler: scrambled eggs, bacon, and toast.

Alan frowned down at it. "Not particularly. I think the cook might be taking a bit of...down time."

Maris realized that without Nadia, the staff had quickly slacked off.

"Well," Mac said, "we'll let you get back to it. The sooner we get this solved, the sooner the ship can get back to normal."

The cinematographer picked up his fork. "Godspeed then."

Apparently Mac had gotten familiar with the layout of the boat yesterday, since he took the stairs to the guest rooms, and then another flight of steps down. For a few moments, a familiar tightness rose in her chest. It seemed like they were descending below the water line, to an area that would be entirely enclosed. An image of the dark elevator leapt into her mind, but Maris gripped the handrail and forced it from her thoughts.

But as they reached the next floor level, Mac made a sharp left, heading to the front of the boat and—impossibly—daylight.

"What is that?" Maris asked.

Mac waggled his eyebrows at her. "The lifestyles of the rich and famous."

The light was coming from an open bay in the side of the yacht. They weren't below the water line at all. In fact, they were still a few feet above it. To her disbelief, they stepped into an amazingly clean white room with an equally clean and white dinghy, suspended in the air in front of them.

"A boat?" Maris whispered, staring at it. "In a boat?"

Lloyd Kunkel appeared from inside a large white control room. "The skiff," he said, wiping his hands off with a rag and smiling. "For day trips, shallow waters, and all-around fun."

Maris gaped at it. As sleek as the yacht itself, it had twin, white outboard engines, and it's inflatable hull was trimmed in silver. The enormous side panel of the yacht was ringed with thick rubber gaskets and raised high in the air outside the hull by two large arms with pistons.

"Wow," Maris said, still not quite sure they were safe with such a huge hole in the side of the boat, "this is amazing."

"Feel free to look around," the first mate said. "Just don't push any buttons."

"Actually," Mac said, "we were looking for you. I have a few questions."

Lloyd's smile slipped a little. "Okay," he said and set the rag aside. "What can I do for you?"

"I understand that the crew had a nickname for Captain Hazelwood," the sheriff said, taking out his note pad. He opened it and looked through a few pages before looking at Lloyd. "Bligh," he said.

Lloyd took a deep breath. "Behind his back, yeah." He glanced at the notepad. "They'd sometimes call him Captain Bligh. It's a standard joke you hear on pretty much every ship."

"And pushing him overboard and calling him lost at sea?" Mac asked.

Lloyd grimaced now. "It's talk. Just talk. The crew needs to blow off steam now and again. I've never been on a ship where they didn't. Most of the time, they'd come to me to vent. I'd listen to their gripes and sympathize, but at the end of the day there's one captain and everyone obeys his orders." He looked between Mac and Maris. "It's the norm, not the exception."

Mac made no comment, but flipped to another page. "I've done a little records search," he said. "It would seem that you've just received your captain's license." He closed the notepad. "Planning on being promoted?"

Lloyd tensed and his lips pressed into a hard line. "Always," he said. "It's part of the job." He glanced out at the white mist beyond the hull. "It takes years of work and study. It's a constant part of the life." He looked at them both. "No one wants to retire as a first mate."

"Fair enough," Mac said. "Why didn't you mention it?"

"Because I'm planning...or I was planning...on leaving *Copernicus*."

"Leave?" Maris said, and looked around at the amazing ship. "Leave all this?"

Mac tucked away his notepad. "Especially when Falschung made you an offer for the captaincy?"

Lloyd cocked his head back. "An offer? Me?"

"We have the offer letter," Mac said. "Signed by him and dated a week ago."

Lloyd shook his head. "I've never seen it." He shook his head again. "No one even knows I passed the exam." When he was met with silence, he said, "Look, I am going to captain a ship. I've worked long and hard for it. But it doesn't have to be *Copernicus*. I wasn't planning on staying."

"Do you spend much time in the sauna?" Mac asked.

The first mate blinked. "The sauna? It's off-limits for the crew." He glanced upward in its direction. "Frankly, not even the guests used it. It was strictly Fritz's thing."

"Did you ever seen anyone in its vicinity?" Maris asked. "Besides Fritz?"

"Of course," Lloyd said. "It was cleaned every day. One of the stewards would have been in there to clean and provide fresh towels."

Maris frowned as she thought back to how Fritz had tossed the towel to the floor in front of Nadia. She might have been in the sauna—at least to inspect that it was clean.

Maris exchanged a look with the sheriff. There didn't seem to be any more questions. Mac said, "I'll let you get back to work, then. Thanks for your time."

"Thank you," Maris said.

"Of course," the first mate replied. But Maris noted that they were leaving him in a decidedly less happy mood than when they'd arrived.

When they'd climbed the stairs back up to the guest room level, Maris said, "He seemed genuinely surprised about the offer from Fritz."

"He did," Mac said, gesturing down the hallway. "My gut says it wasn't him. He might have wanted to see the captain out of the way, but killing Fritz was like killing the goose that laid the golden egg." They arrived at a guest room, and he paused. "But that's not why I don't figure him as the perp."

Maris raised her eyebrows. "No?"

Mac shook his head as he opened the cabin door. "He works too hard. Every time I've seen him, he's working. No matter the city, I've found that crime and hard work don't often go together."

Maris had to laugh a little. "I suppose not."

Only a step into the room, they were both brought up short. It was an utter mess. Two open suitcases sat on the floor, their contents spilling out. High heels and sandals were strewn everywhere. There was even a plate of half eaten fresh fruit on one nightstand.

"Our young actress left in a bit of a rush," Mac said.

"So it would appear," Maris agreed. Nor did the stewards seem to be doing their jobs, now that Nadia wasn't here to oversee them.

Mac handed her a pair of gloves. "I'll take the bathroom and closet."

"I'll start with the nightstands and bed," she replied, putting on the gloves.

The nightstands only held a charger, a packet of tissue, and some magazines. The bed was unmade, the pillows were smashed against the headboard, and the sheets and comforter were completely rumpled.

"Nadia would go nuts," she muttered, since it was already making Maris want to tidy up the bed. But as she scooped up the pillow, her fingers hit something hard. She went still, trying not to move it any more than she had, and picked up the pillows.

"Mac," she called to him. "I think you should see this."

The sheriff immediately strode out of the bathroom, pill bottle in hand.

Maris pointed to the bed. It was a multi-tool.

Mac set down the pills on the nightstand and took an evidence bag from his back pocket. He inverted it, inside out, and picked up the tool. Holding it to the window light, Maris could clearly see what he could: it was full of little hexagonal rods of various lengths and thicknesses, all folded into the middle.

"Good grief," Maris whispered. It had to be the tool that was used on the sauna's doorknob.

Mac sealed the evidence bag. "Let's finish up," he said, putting the bag on the night-stand and picking up the pills.

Several more silent minutes of hunting through the small cabin revealed nothing more. Though Maris had been the one to find the tool, she didn't feel any sense of ac-complishment. Instead a cold dread was set-tling in her stomach. Kaitlyn had seemed completely genuine. But then again, she made her living as an actress.

"I think that's it," Mac said. He pealed off his gloves, tossed them in the trash, and picked up the evidence bag.

Maris did the same. "Now what?"

"Fingerprints first," Mac said, as they exited into the small hallway and climbed the stairs. "Then it might be time for an arrest warrant."

Although Maris frowned, she couldn't object. They'd essentially found the murder weapon. Even so, she couldn't imagine that the young woman was the mind behind two such gruesome murders. She glanced at the point where the lighthouse's beam whirled. As they walked to the gangway along the side of the yacht, Maris thought about the wine and cheese the evening before. Everyone had seemed so at ease.

Only when they reached the platform between *Seas the Day* and *Copernicus* did Maris realize that Slick was watching them. Cookie's parting words came back to her.

"Mac," she said, putting a hand on his arm to stop him. "Would it be all right for Slick to get back to sea?"

Mac stopped and eyed the old mariner. "I seriously doubt he could have snuck aboard the *Copernicus* to loosen a set screw." The sheriff glanced back up at the railing of the yacht. "And it seems evident that Hazelwood was likely shot up on deck, before falling overboard on Slick's boat." He turned back to Maris with a smile. "Sure. I'll let him know."

20

When Maris returned home, it was to a quiet house—until she heard a metal clanking and rattling sound coming from the hallway.

"What in the world?" she muttered, as she set down her purse and headed that way.

It was coming from the open door of the downstairs bathroom. She'd been about to step inside, but stopped so fast that she had to grab the doorjambs to keep from tumbling in.

A big pair of workman's boots blocked her way. They in turn were attached to long legs and a burgeoning stomach, all clad in blue overalls. She saw Bear's big arms, but he was lying on his back with his head under the sink in the cabinet.

"Bear?" she said.

He tried to sit up and Maris heard a thump. "Oops," he said.

Though he couldn't see her, she put out a hand. "It's just me, Bear. It's Maris."

His big hand came out from under the pipes and waved. "Hi, Maris."

"Hi," she said, crouching down, still not able to see his face. "Plumbing problem?"

"The cold water knob was loose," he said, his voice a bit muffled.

"Was," Maris said. "I like the sound of that."

Bear slowly maneuvered an improbable looking tool out from under the sink. It was a long pole with a strange little attachment at the end that looked like a crab claw. She was trying to imagine how it would help, when he started to wriggle out. She stood and backed up as the impossibly big man extricated himself from the too tiny space. As though he was an inch worm, he slowly made his way out from under the sink, then out of the cabinet, his legs projecting diagonally from the door. Finally, with his head clear, he sat up. Small flakes of rust dotted his face and beard, but he smiled at her.

"All done," he said.

"Fabulous," she said. For a moment she nearly extended a hand to help him up, and then realized he'd pull her over. She backed up a pace. "*Thank you.*"

"You're welcome," he said, and then with an amazing nimbleness that belied his size, he simply got to his feet and brushed off his face and beard.

Without the metal clanking, Maris realized how quiet the house was. "Where is everyone?" she asked.

Bear stooped to pick up his tools. "Cookie is taking a nap. The older couple said they were going to take pictures of flowers. The other women are kayaking. I think they called it a jaunt."

Maris grinned a little. That sounded like Nadia. She was glad that her friend was relaxing, although she'd hoped to speak with Kaitlyn about what Mac and she had found.

"Is there something you need done, Maris?" Bear said.

Something? Maris thought. She had a whole list. She lived by her lists. "Nothing in particular," she said.

It'd always been a sore spot for her that,

in the hospitality trade, the doers were always rewarded with more things to be done. Now that she ran her own establishment, she wasn't going to make the same mistake.

"You say no," Bear said, still holding his tools. "But your voice says yes."

Maris was never quite sure what to make of the big handyman. He'd finally overcome his shyness around her, and they were having longer conversations. But it didn't change his awkwardness, or the simple and very direct way he had of phrasing things. Either he was a man of very few words, or a sage in the guise of bib overalls.

"Come on," she said, heading to the front rooms. "I'll show you." She exited onto the back porch, where the sun had broken through and the last of the mist was dissipating. "This is something I've been thinking about for a while, that doesn't have to do with the usual upkeep." She used her hand to shade her eyes as she looked up to the sky. "I'm wondering if we can go solar."

He shaded his eyes and looked up as well. "Solar panels," he said. "There's lots of sun."

Maris nodded. "That's what I was thinking. But we'd need to have batteries for when it's foggy or cloudy." She gazed at the lighthouse. "We could have them in there, I guess, but I don't know where the panels themselves would go. I don't want to spoil the Victorian look."

"Let's see," he said, stepping off the porch. He walked for several paces and stopped at Cookie's herb garden. He pointed to its center. "Here."

Maris had to gawk at him. If anyone so much as touched a leaf in that garden, Cookie would have a fit.

He broke into a grin. "Just kidding."

Maris put a hand over her heart and laughed. "You got me." He really was getting less shy.

But as she followed him around the back and to the south side of the house, he pointed upward. "Here." She followed his gaze to the roof. "You can't see it except from the lighthouse."

She looked from the roof up to Claribel's optic house, then from the roof toward the front of the property. It was true. This part of the many gabled roof couldn't be seen except from where they stood, and the lighthouse.

"It's a good solution," she told him. Then

she put her hands on her hips. "It'd be nice not to have to rely on the grid."

He put his hands in his pockets. "It's never failed."

Maris frowned a little. That was true. She gazed up at the lighthouse. With their emergency generator and the deep-cycle batteries, the Old Girl had never missed a day. Maris looked back to the roof. Was she making work just for the sake of doing it? Solving a problem that didn't exist?

But when she looked back to Bear, he was looking out to sea. He pointed at something. "There they are."

She could barely make out two small dots the color of orange life preserver vests bobbing on white smudges in the far distance. That had to be Nadia and Kaitlyn on the kayaks. "What good eyes you've got," Maris exclaimed.

"Time to mow the lawn," Bear said.

As though the discussion of the solar panels had just been a little blip in the day, he simply walked off toward the detached garage where the tools were stored. Maris had to smile as she watched him go. The solar panels were indeed a blip.

But as she looked back to sea, it took a minute for her to find the dots and smudges. It'd likely be some time before Nadia and Kaitlyn were back, and Maris could ask the actress some questions. She glanced back at Claribel. Maybe the Old Girl could help.

21

Just before Maris reached the door to the conical tower, a gust of ocean air seemed to blow the door open. With a smile, Maris wondered if was just her imagination, or if the Old Girl knew she was coming.

Inside, she flipped on the light switch and said, "Good morning, Claribel."

In response, the door gently blew closed behind her.

Maris began the long climb upward, pacing herself. As a child, she'd delighted in racing Aunt Glenda to the top. Now, she just wanted to make it without soaking her clothes with sweat. But step by step, up the spiraling metal staircase, she slowly scaled the three stories. Finally, at the top, she was moving at a snail's pace and breathing hard.

By the time she took the last step out onto the metal landing, she had to stop.

"Phew!" she exhaled as she paused for a moment taking in the view and catching her breath.

The bay and the sea beyond it sparkled in bright green tones of peridot and emerald. Maris could see the kayaks clearly now, without the ocean's haze at ground level. She could even see the difference between Nadia's dark hair and the blonde of Kaitlyn's. To the north, the pier jutted out from the land like little matchsticks, but the long white yacht was visible against it. Though Maris could probably stand there drinking in the view for hours, she'd come for a reason. She turned to the fresnel lens.

It was more like a glass sculpture than something one would imagine in binoculars or a telescope. Shaped almost like a giant egg, dozens of individual pieces of glass, some grooved with concentric circles, were tightly fitted together on a gleaming steel frame. It rose from its waist high pedestal up to nearly the top of the circular glass house.

Its thousands of reflective surfaces bounced light in every direction, and it glowed as though it had a life of its own. The beam was off, as it typically was in the day, when the light sensor was triggered to shut off both the turning mechanism and the LEDs.

"How are you today, Claribel?" Maris asked and gazed down into the faceted base of the lens. Sunlight danced within it like a prism, tossing out flecks of kaleidoscope light that were mesmerizing. Then an image began to form among the sparkles.

It was like looking through a telescope at the...utility room? Previously, Claribel had shown her images of places in town or elsewhere, but never her own B&B. But as she watched, the vision zoomed in to focus on the wooden door in the floor that Maris knew led to the basement.

Despite having made it to the top of the tower without breaking into a sweat, Maris felt her palms grow damp and a trickle in the small of her back. She'd been meaning to investigate the basement and continue her search for Aunt Glenda's pendulum, but her mild claustrophobia had prevented that. Maris's eyes narrowed. Was Claribel telling her that something to do with the murders was in the basement?

But as quickly as the image had popped into view, it vanished. Though she waited for another few moments, hoping against hope that the basement was not the message, the remote viewing was over.

"Thank you," she said, sighing heavily, and gave the pedestal an affectionate pat before beginning her descent.

22

___

In her room, Maris stared at the skeleton key hanging on the hook. When she'd first come back to Pixie Point Bay, she'd found it in Aunt Glenda's silk brocade boudoir box. Along with it, there'd been some paperwork: the will and life insurance policy, the deeds to the lighthouse and the B&B, property insurance and various warranties. But it had also held a small box that Maris had recognized. It had once contained a faceted green stone in the shape of an inverted cone that hung on a silver chain. Although she'd always wanted to wear it, Aunt Glenda had said that it wasn't meant to be worn. It wasn't a pendant but rather a pendulum. To Maris it didn't matter what it was.

Pendant or no, it would still make a nice necklace.

But when she'd opened the little box, it was empty.

Though she'd searched her room many times, even moving furniture, it had never turned up. Of course she'd thought about finding it in the basement, especially since the skeleton key to the door had been in the boudoir box. But she had yet to work up the nerve to go down there. Now it seemed that a clue about the murders might be down below.

Maris glared at the ominous black key on the hook next to the door. She had to un-clench her hand to reach for it.

"I hope you're right, Claribel," she muttered, grasping the key.

Reluctantly, she went to the back of her room, opened the door to the utility room, and stepped inside. There in the floor was the door to the basement, it's heavy black hinges and handle matching the antique lock.

It had perhaps been inevitable that, in her journey from one troubled hotel property to another, that Maris had found one with an improperly maintained elevator. Though the mechanics had later assured her that she'd never been in any real danger, the three hours spent alone in darkness and uncertainty had left its imprint. Though she'd always been glad for her photographic memory, the images from that time in the elevator ensured she never forgot it.

When she inserted the large key into the lock, she found that it rattled—but only because her hand shook. Using two hands, she cranked the key in the sturdy mechanism and heard the familiar grating and clunking she remembered from when Aunt Glenda would open it. With a final click, the key moved freely and Maris grasped the handle of the hatch.

You don't have to go down, she told herself. *Just open it.*

With a tug, she lifted the heavy wood door and looked down.

A rhythmic thumping sounded behind her, quickly drawing closer, and Maris yelped a little as a little black cat flew past her and down the wood stairs.

"Mojo," she exclaimed, nearly dropping the door closed. With an effort, she shoved it

all the way open and lay it on the floor—then took a deep breath. "You're lucky I didn't lock you in," she called down to him. The cat was infuriating—and she was *so* glad to have his company. "Don't get lost down there."

Slowly, she took her first step down, and then the next.

Your head's still above ground level. You can do this.

Another couple steps had the floor at waist level. She reached down to the wall just inside and was relieved to find the light switch. She turned it on.

The fluorescent light in the ceiling below made a little tinking sound, then the light fluttered, and came on. Maris blew out a breath.

"Good," she muttered. The room below was far less intimidating when it was lit.

At the bottom of the steps was the familiar brick floor. Maris couldn't count the times she'd come here with her aunt. Like Mojo, she'd run down the stairs, eager to find some new treasure among all the old trunks. But now to her astonishment, there was something new. A diagonal bookcase built into the wall flanked the stairs. It ran parallel, all the way down. There had to be at least a dozen shelves, all full, and one with a little black cat sitting on it.

"What have you found?" she asked him.

Without thinking, she descended another couple steps and realized she was looking at what seemed to be a small library. Most of the volumes appeared to be antique books but there were also some leather bound journals. The beautiful spines gleamed with gold lettering, and one title in particular caught her eye.

"Magick Folk," she read. She glanced back to the utility room door. No one was there. She gave the open hatch a firm pat to make sure it wouldn't move. Then she went down another few steps and took a seat, before she withdrew the oversize book and opened it.

Though the edges of the pages had colored with age, the paper was in excellent condition. After flipping through a few pages, Maris realized what she'd found: an encyclopedia. Everything was arranged alphabetically. She went immediately to Precognition.

Apparently this magical talent could manifest differently. Some witches had brief flashes that included sight, sound, and even smell. Maris smiled to herself—not that she'd doubted Cookie. But to see her own talent here in black and white... It seemed more real, more normal. Eagerly, she turned back to Potions.

Maris had to smile at the description of herb gardens and the tonics and tissons they produced, designed to be exactly what a person might need at that particular moment.

Then another thought occurred to her and she flipped to the index at the back. There was no entry for fishing, nor any for boating. But near the end of all the listings was one for Water Elemental. There she read about a type of magic folk that could not only manipulate water in all its forms, but also held a special bond with it. Using that bond, they could direct its flow as well as the creatures who lived within it.

She tapped on the page with her index finger. "Slick," she said grinning. She'd been about to look up more entries when she heard footsteps in the house, and then female voices. Quickly, she put the book back, picked up Mojo, and headed back up the stairs. She turned off the light switch and, after setting Mojo on the floor, climbed all the way out and closed the heavy door over. With a bit of relief, and not a small amount of satisfaction, she turned the key in the lock and heard the tumblers fall into place.

23

Maris followed the sound of the voices and found Nadia and Kaitlyn, still in their shorts and tank tops, sitting in the living room. They both grinned as Maris entered. She studied them both for a moment.

"Kayaking agrees with you," she declared, smiling. "I prescribe one kayaking trip per day."

Nadia laughed and clapped her hands. "I can do that."

"It really was the most relaxing thing," Kaitlyn gushed. She looked at Nadia. "We have to remember to let the Magnusons know and thank them. They really nailed it."

"Oh yes," Nadia agreed, then beamed at Maris. "And all courtesy of the best B&B that

I've ever come across." She glanced around at the Victorian furnishings, and then out the window up the coast. "It really is just perfect."

"Thank you," Maris said sincerely. "That means a lot coming from you."

"Were you at the yacht this morning?" Kaitlyn asked. "I think Cookie said you were headed there."

Maris nodded. "I was."

"How's the crew doing?" Nadia asked.

"As far as I could tell," Maris answered, "very well." She decided to skip how meals and room service on the yacht had changed since her departure.

"Good," Nadia said. Though she opened her mouth as if she had another question, she closed it. "Good," she repeated, then took a deep breath. "Dibs on the shower," she told Kaitlyn as she stood.

"Go for it," Kaitlyn said, sitting back. "I'm fine right here."

When Nadia left, Maris took a seat, grateful not to have asked for a private conversation. She decided to come directly to the point.

"We searched your room this morning," Maris said.

Kaitlyn grimaced a bit. "Sorry about the mess."

"I'm not worried about the mess," Maris replied.

Kaitlyn cocked her head, her brows drawing together. "Are you worried about something else?"

Maris studied the young actress. Was she playing a part? "We found a screwdriver under your pillow. They're also called allen wrenches."

For a moment, the words didn't register. Then she said, "A screwdriver?" Her eyebrows flew up. "A screwdriver under my pillow?" She sat forward on the chair. "I don't own a screwdriver," she blurted out. "I don't have one. Why would I put one under my pillow?"

Maris held up her hand to stop her. "It was the same tool used to loosen the set screw on the sauna's doorknob."

Kaitlyn shot to her feet. "Sauna? Wait. What's a set screw?" She'd broken out in a sweat and her upper lip glistened. "What are you saying?" Her voice was getting louder and high-pitched. "Oh my god. *What's a set screw?*"

Maris maintained an even tone. "It keeps the doorknob from falling off. Someone loosened it to keep Fritz in the sauna."

Kaitlyn took a step back, eyes wide and her jaw dropped open. She held up both her hands. "Wait. You think that I killed Fritz?" She shook her head so hard that her hair tossed one way and then the other. "No way," she said, her voice trembling. "No way." She stared at Maris. "He was going to make me a star," she said, her voice pleading now. "I was going to be in his next movie."

"All right," Maris said soothingly as she stood. "Take it easy, and try to calm down."

Kaitlyn visibly tried to do just that, taking a deep breath, and closing her eyes. "Okay," she muttered, then opened her eyes. "I do not know anything about any screwdriver. I swear it."

Maris inclined her head. Either Kaitlyn was telling the truth or she'd just seen an Oscar winning performance. "I believe you."

Kaitlyn flopped back down in the chair. "Oh my god," she whispered. "This is so awful. It was supposed to be a fun cruise."

"I know," Maris said, her voice full of the sympathy that she really felt.

Kaitlyn shook her head. "A screwdriver under my pillow," she muttered. She looked into Maris's eyes. "What does the sheriff think?"

Maris gave her a reassuring smile. "He doesn't jump to conclusions. He's having it fingerprinted."

For the first time since the conversation started, Kaitlyn actually smiled a little. "Oh thank goodness. Because it will *not* have my fingerprints on it."

24

At the top of the stairs, Maris heard Nadia out on the side balcony, on the south side of the Victorian home. It sounded like she was talking. Kaitlyn had followed her upstairs but crossed straight to the bathroom and peeked inside.

"Good," the young actress said. "I need to soak my head under a good hot shower."

Maris watched her go to her room before she turned to the sunny balcony. Nadia was on the phone, but said, "Gotta go," and hung up. She beckoned for Maris to join her, and showed her the phone. "Just checking on the crew."

"How are they?" Maris asked, coming to the railing. The view to the south took in the jagged coast, its verdant hills rising above the rocky points that fronted the sea.

"Good," Nadia said, putting the phone in her back pocket. Her sleek black hair was still damp, but she'd changed into jeans and a blouse. She hadn't done her makeup, but then again, she didn't really need it. "It seems to me that the last I heard, you were in Hong Kong."

Maris looked across the ocean in that direction. "You heard right."

Nadia leaned on the railing with her elbows. "Then how did you end up here? It's an awfully long way from those glittering resorts where we used to work."

Maris told her the story of Aunt Glenda and her sudden death. Coming from so far, she'd arrived too late for the funeral. But she and Cookie had fallen into a routine of sorts, even in those first early days. It just seemed natural. And since Glenda had not had children of her own, Maris had inherited the B&B and the lighthouse.

"I'd spent so much time here," Maris said, "that it just felt like home, so I decided to stay." She smiled at her friend. "Not much of a decision really."

"No, not really," Nadia agreed. "It can all be such a grind sometimes."

Maris looked at her. "So you don't like your job?"

Nadia frowned a little and tilted her head. "I do and I don't. You know what I've decided?" Maris shook her head. "It's the small fries that are the worst. The ones who aren't really that famous—but want to be."

Maris laughed a little. "It doesn't change then, land or sea."

Nadia rolled her eyes. "We had some composer on board on a 'special diet'." She used air quotes. "He needed six small meals per day, and each one had to be prepared according to his nutritionist's guidelines. Then one day in port, he'd been shopping ashore and dropped his bag coming up the gangway. Three candy bars, a bag of potato chips, and beef jerky spilled out. I could have throttled him right there and then."

Maris laughed. "Good grief. I'd have served him *that*, six times a day."

As their laughter died down, Maris said, "But Fritz Falschung. He couldn't have been that easy to work for, the way he threw that towel on the floor in front of you."

Nadia shrugged. "You know the type," was all she said.

"And the captain? Hazelwood? I've yet to hear something genuinely nice about him."

"Ugh," Nadia said. "Captain Bligh we called him. But what was really insufferable was the way the two of them warred. It was some kind of strange competition to see who could be more demanding. 'There's only one wheel on a ship, because there's only one captain.' I can't count the number of times I heard that from Hazelwood."

"The first time I met Fritz," Maris said, "he was wearing a captain's hat. It seemed a little ridiculous."

"Petty is what I'd call it," her former colleague said.

"How did the captain manage to keep his job then? I assume Fritz could have fired him and hired someone else."

Nadia acknowledged that with a nod. "Mind you, I haven't been aboard for a long time, but from what I can gather, Hazelwood was safe. He'd prided himself on having no accidents of any sort." Nadia looked down the coast. "It's hard to argue with safety. Sometimes out there, in the middle of the ocean, you realize how much your life depends on the sailors knowing how to do their jobs."

As Maris was considering how difficult that might be, she heard a car on the drive and recognized the Magnuson's SUV.

25

Maris and Nadia headed downstairs as the Magnusons came in from their day out. Dressed in their hiking outfits and carrying their broad hats, they wore big smiles as well.

"Good afternoon," Maris said with a smile. "Looks like you've had another successful adventure."

"Oh it was wonderful," Gayle said, camera slung over her shoulder.

"Couldn't have asked for better weather," Mark agreed.

"I can't wait to hear all about it," Maris said, but tilted her head in the direction of the kitchen. "But I think I hear a pitcher of lemonade calling our names. Hold that thought?"

Mark grinned as he clasped his hands and rubbed them together. "Holding."

As he and Gayle moved to the living room, Nadia said, "Can I help you?"

After a moment's hesitation, she said, "That'd be great."

If this morning's kayaking had shown anything, it was how taking a break had done Nadia a world of good. But at the same time, Maris knew that part of what made them both good at hospitality was having a genuine desire to provide it.

In the kitchen Maris took a loaf of gingerbread that Cookie had baked from the refrigerator and set it on the counter.

"If you want to cut a few slices of this," Maris told Nadia, "I'll get the pitcher and glasses."

In short order, they were able to bring two trays to the living room, where they found that Kaitlyn had joined the Magnusons. Maris was relieved to find her smiling and seemingly back to her old self.

"I was just telling Gayle and Mark about our kayaking," the young actress said to Nadia, who set down the gingerbread.

"It was as easy as you said," she agreed, "and we had a truly marvelous time."

Nadia used a pair of tongs and put a slice of gingerbread on a small plate. "Gingerbread?" she said, offering it to Gayle.

The older woman's eyes lit up as she took it. "Why, it looks homemade." She broke off a bit and tasted it. "Oh, it *has* to be homemade."

As Maris poured a lemonade and handed it to Mark, she said, "Cookie is that rare combination of chef and baker. They don't always go together."

Nadia had to laugh a little. "To be sure," she said offering a slice to Mark.

"Just half a slice for me," Kaitlyn said, when Nadia turned to her.

In another few minutes, everyone had their lemonade and afternoon snack. In an effort to battle the bulge, Maris opted for just a glass of lemonade—a perfectly thirst quenching one. Standing next to the fireplace, she smiled a little to herself. You could always count on Cookie.

"What have you two been doing today?" Nadia asked the older couple, as she took a seat.

Gayle hefted her camera. "I couldn't resist the Pixie Point Petal Farms. What a complete and joyous riot of color." She put down her lemonade. "Care to see?"

"Well, with that kind of endorsement," Nadia said, "I can hardly wait."

Gayle turned on the camera and, even from where Maris stood, she could see that the screen on the back was bathed in the rich colors of rows upon rows of flowers.

The older woman handed it to Nadia, who sat next to Kaitlyn on the settee. "Just hit that button to scroll through." Maris came to stand behind them as Nadia began to look through the images.

"Stunning," Nadia murmured.

"Oh look at that," Kaitlyn gasped.

As with her photos in the redwoods, Gayle had captured up close and panoramic views that were simply astonishing. In one image, a striped sea of tulips stretched to the horizon. In the next, dew clung to the petals of a white flower but each watery orb held a tiny image of a flower behind it.

"Wow," Nadia and Kaitlyn whispered together.

"One thing Gayle hasn't mentioned,"

Maris said, giving the older woman a wink, "is that she's a professional."

"Ah," Nadia said, nodding, but still scrolling through the images. "I should have guessed."

"Retired," Gayle added after she finished a sip of her lemonade.

"But never better," Mark tacked on, and his wife playfully batted his arm.

Kaitlyn pointed at the screen. "Aww, who are these kids?"

Maris peered down at the image. Two freckle-faced girls seemed to be hiding behind a wall of red flowers. Sunlight glinted off their curly auburn hair, and seemed to dance in their blue eyes.

"They're adorable," Nadia said.

Mark took another slice of gingerbread. "We ran into a few families there." He craned his neck to look at the camera screen before he sat back down. "They were picking some flowers for a bouquet for their mom when Gayle spotted the shot."

"Oh, are these the farmers?" Kaitlyn asked. Various men and women in big straw hats, long sleeved shirts, and gloves held baskets full of freshly picked blooms. Their ready smiles as they stood among the rows really made it seem as though they loved what they were doing.

"Yes," Gayle said. "That particular farm was a family owned business."

Maris went back to the fireplace. "You could shoot their business brochure," she said. "Or at least take some shots for their web site."

"Wait a minute," Kaitlyn said, reaching to her back pocket. "I've got some photos." She took out her camera. "And I wonder if I could get your opinion."

She swiped to the photos that Alan had taken of her, and handed the phone to Gayle. Mark leaned in closer for a look as well.

"I need a new head shot," she said, and glanced at Maris, "especially since it seems I'll be out auditioning soon." She sighed a little before she looked over to the older couple. "Fritz's cinematographer shot these. What do you think? Is there one that's better than the others?"

But as Gayle swiped from one photo to the next, and then back to the beginning, she didn't say a word. Instead she frowned, and

Kaitlyn looked from Nadia to Maris and then back to Gayle.

"Am I that unphotogenic?" she asked.

Maris picked up the pitcher and poured for everyone all around.

Gayle shook her head. "You're as pretty as the day is long. But maybe cinematography is different than still photography. If it were me, I wouldn't use any of these."

Although Maris had been about to fetch more lemonade from the kitchen, she stopped.

Kaitlyn frowned as she held out her hand for the phone. "None of them?"

Gayle stood up, and brought the phone to the young actress so they both could look. "Here," she said, pointing to the image. "You're backlit. The sun on the water is so bright, that your face has fallen into shadow."

"But," Kaitlyn said, studying it, "isn't that always how these kinds of shots look?"

"Oh no," Gayle replied. "Having a photo that looks natural means never actually doing what is natural." She pointed to the face in the image. "This needed some fill flash, or a bounce from a reflector." When Kaitlyn shook her head, Gayle added, "Your face needed some extra light." Then the photographer swiped to the next one. "Poor composition," she said. "Your eyes should be on one of the golden thirds." She went to the next image. "These little hexagons of yellow? That's lens flare."

"Oh," Kaitlyn said, "I thought that was pretty."

"It is," Gayle agreed, "if that's what you want. But I wouldn't recommend it in a portrait."

As the retired photographer continued, Maris got a tingling feeling along her spine. Cinematography and photography were different, but that different? As she listened to Gayle's analysis, Maris thought that any one of them could have done a better job. It was as if Alan hadn't really cared about how they came out.

Maris went still.

She picked up the empty pitcher. "I'll be right back."

26

Once Maris was in the kitchen and sure that she was alone, she tapped her temple and brought up an image of the script she'd seen on Fritz's tablet. She flipped past the initial pages, where the text was all black. When some of it became blue, she paused. When they'd searched his room, she hadn't really concentrated on the details of the manuscript. It'd just struck her as interesting that people who 'gave notes' as Kaitlyn put it, would get different color fonts.

But now she wondered if that just wasn't how the software worked. Did anybody really take time to color their notes? She examined the margins of the document as well. Yes, as she suspected, there were Fritz's initials, FF.

Not only did the software keep track of the different contributors, it knew who they were. Toward the end of the document were more initials that she recognized.

She glanced at the clock on the microwave. There might be enough time.

Trying to be quiet, she hurried back to her room, found her phone, and called Slick.

"Hello?" he answered, with the type of inquisitiveness in his voice that said he didn't often get called.

Maris shut the door to her room. "Slick? It's Maris. Are you at the pier?" She strode to the bay window looking at the low slant of the afternoon sun.

"Yup," he said. "Just finishing up with the oil change. I'll head out in the morning. Thanks for putting a bug in the sheriff's ear."

"You're welcome," she said quickly. "Can you meet me at the yacht in say, an hour?"

"*Copernicus*?" he asked, as though she'd asked him to clean a latrine. "What's this about?"

"I'll tell you in an hour," she said. "I've got to go. See you then."

When she hung up, she dialed Mac's number.

27

That evening, as the sun sank toward the horizon, no one took notice. Although the view from the aft deck of the yacht was ideal, particularly for a panorama of the bay, everyone was turned to face Maris. The first mate was looking apprehensive, and his crew looked bored. The guests, Alan and Kaitlyn, sat next to each other and exchanged a few whispers. Nadia sat quietly with the crew, next to Lloyd. Slick leaned against the railing, pipe in mouth, but unlit. His thick white eyebrows waggled at her as though he was ready for the show to begin. The sheriff, who stood at her side, nodded to her.

"Thank you, everyone," Maris began, "for meeting us here."

Although she paused for a moment and looked around the circle, no one uttered a word. Like her, they seemed ready to have this over.

"As you all know, I first became involved when the body of Captain Hazelwood was found on the deck of Slick Duff's boat." She indicated *Seas the Day*. "But as we've suspected from the start, the captain wasn't killed there."

Slick took the pipe from his mouth. "I could have told you that." Then he thought for a moment. "Didn't I tell you that?"

Maris smiled at the old man. "You were at the warehouse processing your catch. The body was on your boat the next morning when you got back."

Slick nodded and pointed his pipe at her. "That's when I picked up the flare gun."

"Right," she said. "And that's when you were seen."

Lloyd spoke up. "If the gun and body were on his boat, doesn't it make sense that's where the captain was shot?" He glanced at Slick. "Even if Captain Duff didn't do it?"

Mac shook his head. "The forensics team swabbed both ships." He indicated the long deck on the yacht next to Slick's boat. "Residue from the flare's cartridge was all over the deck, not *Seas the Day*."

"So the body fell overboard," Maris concluded. "It'd seemed that way from the start, but the lab work confirmed it."

"So the Captain was killed on *Copernicus*," Nadia said. "By someone here."

The entire group looked around at each other.

"Correct," Maris said, and looked at Kaitlyn.

It took a few moments for everyone to follow her gaze, but when Kaitlyn realized they were all looking at her, she quickly said, "No!" She looked from the sheriff to Maris and then back again. "I told you. I was in my room posting to my fans."

"And it's true that your social media posts coincide with the murder time," Mac agreed. "But it's also true that you can schedule social media posts ahead of time. The time stamps on those posts don't mean anything."

Kaitlyn threw up her hands. "I have no idea how to do that," she protested. "I hardly know how my phone works. Ask anyone here."

To that there were several nods from the group, and Maris had to suppress a smile.

"When Falschung was asked for an alibi," the sheriff continued. "He said that you were in his room. All night."

Although Kaitlyn grimaced and shook her head, she didn't protest.

"Is it true?" Maris asked her. "Were you with him at the time of the murder?"

The young actress crossed her arms over her chest. "No, it's not," she said and looked at the deck. "But that's what he thought."

Maris cocked her head at her. "I'm sorry. What?"

Kaitlyn glared at her. "He passed out drunk, okay? And I left." She looked defiantly around the assembled group. "He passed out every night. The jerk even thought he was sleeping with me. But every night, like clockwork, he got drunk, took his pills, and passed out. Then I left. He was always in a foul mood in the morning, so I made sure to be long gone."

Maris and Mac exchanged a look. They'd certainly found that was true.

Maris turned to Lloyd next, but he simply shook his head. "We might not have liked

'Captain Bligh'," he said, drawing a couple of snickers from two of the crew. He shot them a glare that made them stop. "But we were not out to murder him. The same for Mr. Falschung. We had a vested interest in seeing him alive." He gestured to the uniformed people standing near him. "We're essentially without jobs now." Although the snickering crew members had been smiling, they suddenly stopped and looked at one another.

"Also," Nadia said, "Lloyd has an alibi." She took his hand and looked back at Maris. "We were together when Hazelwood was killed."

Maris only nodded. When Fritz had said that fraternization among the crew wasn't permitted, she'd assumed that Nadia was involved. The fact that Lloyd had insisted that she and Kaitlyn leave for their own safety had been the clincher.

"We're going to be married," the first mate said, and smiled at her. "Now that I've got my captain's license, we're going to work for a charter yacht line."

"We'll see the world together," Nadia said to him.

"Which brings me to Fritz," Maris said,

"the only intended victim on this ship."

"What?" Kaitlyn muttered. "But Hazelwood died first."

Maris nodded her agreement. "And here we are, out on deck, at about the same time he was murdered." She gestured to the sunset behind her. "The light is beginning to wane, and I am backlit."

"The murderer had been looking at the captain from behind," Mac said. "He'd shot him in the back."

"But at this time of day," Maris said, "and from the back, when the captain wore his white uniform and cap...."

Nadia gasped. "They both had white hair."

"And short white beards," Maris said. "From the back, they would have looked identical. Fritz in his white dinner jacket and captain's hat would have been indistinguishable from the captain."

Mac looked around the circle. "Captain Hazelwood was never the intended victim. He was killed by mistake. Fritz Falschung had been the murder's target, right from the start."

Maris gazed at Alan. "It must have been

hard for you to tell the two men apart." She squinted against the light behind her. "The gleam of the sun on the water is blinding right now. The captain must have been in silhouette." She turned back to Alan. "You know what silhouette means? I know a cinematographer should, but then again, you're not a cinematographer are you, Alan?"

The big man smirked at her. "What a pretty story you tell. Maybe you should write for Hollywood."

"Ah," Maris said, "but that's your job, isn't it, Alan?" She glanced at Kaitlyn. "What did you call it when someone rewrites a script? A script doctor?"

Kaitlyn could only stare at the man next to her. Then scooted away.

He glowered at her. "Did you know Fritz had been stealing your little ideas for two years?"

"What?" she said. "Mine?"

Alan laughed. "Why do you think you 'shared the same vision'?" The big man made a rude sound. "The genius director didn't have a clue about story. He could barely direct." He looked around the circle of faces staring blankly at him. "That was his *modus operandi*. He didn't need notes. He had no idea what to do with them. He just took other people's ideas and passed them off as his own." He turned back to Maris. "And then I'd rewrite them all into a script."

"But you never got the credit," Maris said. "And I suspect, not the money." She gestured to the yacht all around them. "At least not this kind of money."

"He was a greedy pig," Alan said, sounding as if he could spit. "And vain. A freaking narcissist. No one could know that he used a script doctor. No one could know that I was the story genius, not him." Suddenly, Alan stopped. He grinned at Maris. "So, storyteller. Do you have more than that? Do you have any proof?"

"The offer letter that Kaitlyn found," Mac said, "had no fingerprints. The fortuitous piece of evidence that implicated Lloyd was on the company stationary—which anyone would have had access to."

"The allen wrenches had no fingerprints either," Maris said. "Anyone could have secretly gone to the tool crib, used it, and then put it under Kaitlyn's pillow during the hubbub after Fritz's death."

"Well, then," Alan said, getting up.

Mac stepped forward. "But only one person is going to have residue from the flare gun all over their clothes." He looked down at Alan's feet. "Particularly their shoes. In fact, it's going to be all over their cabin."

Alan's mouth dropped open a little as he stared at his shoes, then the deck around them. "But that's not proof," he whispered. "That's–"

Mac took out his handcuffs. "That's for a jury to decide." He moved behind the big man and brought both wrists behind him. Maris heard the metal ratchet of the cuffs closing.

"But combined with what you just told us all," Maris said, "I doubt the jury will have much trouble."

As Mac escorted Alan from the sitting area he paused in front of Maris. "'Revenge is sweet and not fattening.' I guess he was wrong."

Maris blinked at him. "Robert Burns, wrong?"

"No," Mac said, smiling. "Not Rabbie, Alfred Hitchcock."

28

The next morning, after the Magnusons had finished their breakfast and said their goodbyes, Maris had helped Cookie with the cleanup. As they'd loaded the last plate into the dishwasher, Cookie looked up at the time.

"You don't want to miss them," the chef said.

"Oh goodness," Maris said, drying off her hands on her apron. "Time got away from me."

Cookie's eyebrows rose, but then she smiled with satisfaction. "Good," was all she said.

Maris found Mojo still on her bed and picked him up. "Let's go," she whispered into the soft fur between his ears.

As she took the little cat through the utility room and into the lighthouse, she checked her watch. Slick had said he'd be waiting for the *Copernicus* to leave port, and Lloyd had said that would be at ten.

With the little black cat purring against her side, she slowly and steadily climbed the spiral stairs. The fog was only a thin mist at this point, and the views out the windows at the first two levels showed glimpses of a bright blue sea.

At the top, stepping onto the metal platform of the optics room, Maris gratefully took a break. Breathing hard, she checked the bay in front of the lighthouse and smiled. She was not a moment too soon.

"There they are," she said to Mojo, who seemed to be staring intently.

Seas the Day was escorting *Copernicus* from Pixie Point Bay. Their bows sliced the water, leaving white wakes in their passage. Three short toots of Slick's horn, were followed by one from the yacht.

Grinning, Maris waved her arm in a giant arc, and saw Kaitlyn wave from the upper deck. The young actress had deemed travel by boat as the cheapest way to get home.

From just outside the bridge, she saw Lloyd and Nadia too. She gave an extra wave to her former colleague and her fiancé, who waved back.

"Safe travels," she said, while Mojo gave them his rather loud but signature meow.

"Is that for the boats," she asked him, "or the salmon?"

After what she'd read in the *Magick Folk* encyclopedia, she had no doubt that—with their water elemental on the high seas—Pixie Point Bay would soon be up to its gunnels in fresh fish.

But as she petted Mojo, she recalled his tarot spread. The High Priestess had been concealing a scroll. Had that been a clue about Alan, the secret script doctor? The little cat had also spelled 'yacht' twice on the Ouija board. Had he been trying to warn her about the second murder to take place there?

As she watched the two boats make there way through the tranquil bay and out to the ocean beyond, she wondered for a moment where Nadia and Lloyd would go. She recalled the many wonderful photographs of exotic locales that decorated the yacht, but felt not a twinge of envy. Perhaps one day a picture of her lighthouse, overlooking the sparkling bay, might hang alongside them. Maris had to smile at the thought, because if it did, she knew it'd outshine them all.

Another Pixie Point Bay book awaits you in The Witch Who Filled in the Picture (Pixie Point Bay Book 3).

For a sneak peek, turn the page.

The Witch Who Filled in the Picture

Excerpt

CHAPTER ONE

"Ms. Seaver," someone called, loud enough to be heard above the din.

Inklings New & Used Books, the large three-story store on the Towne Plaza, was positively packed. Maris turned and peered into the crowd, and saw Mikhail Galkin hurrying toward her, both hands outstretched.

"I am delighted you could make it," he said, with just a hint of an exotic Russian accent. He grasped both her hands and, cheek to cheek, gave her an air kiss on one side, and then the other. "Thank you so much for coming."

"I wouldn't have missed it for the world, Mr. Galkin," she told him. "It's not every day we have an international art exhibit in Pixie Point Bay."

Tall, with sandy brown hair and a goatee to match, Maris guessed that he was in his mid-forties. He was looking very smart this evening in his tailored blue blazer and lavender turtleneck.

"*Please*," he said, "call me Mikhail. When you say 'Mr. Galkin', I expect to turn around and see my father." Then he gave her a wry smile. "Although in truth, he was Comrade Galkin."

Maris laughed a little. "Very well, Mikhail. Then I must insist you call me Maris."

From the beginning of his stay at the B&B, the art dealer had been a bit formal. She'd chalked it up to cultural differences, or perhaps that she owned the B&B and attached lighthouse. But here, at his temporary art exhibit, he seemed very much in his element.

He dropped her hands, bowed his head,

and clicked his heels. "Of course, Maris," he said grinning. "Now, may I show you the exhibit?"

"That would be wonderful," she said, smiling and inclining her head.

As they made their way among the many bookshelves and people, Maris was glad she'd spent a little extra time picking her wardrobe. Although it was evening, most of the attendees wore business casual attire, as did she. Her black silk skirt with its small white floral print fell well below the knee, and matched her ruffled white blouse with black trim at the cuffs. The patent black heels were stylish, but low enough to be comfortable for the standing and walking she was anticipating.

Maris recognized a number of the people who were mingling with their plastic cups of wine. Long-time residents and shopkeepers mixed with the usual compliment of tourists, but the upscale dress of several people carrying the exhibit catalog spoke to prospective buyers.

The bookstore's existing recessed lighting was bright and cheery, although Maris spotted extra spot lamps that had been brought in—some with colored film over their fronts. Interestingly they weren't necessarily pointed at the artwork, but highlighted different parts of the ceiling with washes of color.

Mikhail made his way to the edge of the room and the large easels that were lined up in front of the books.

"First," he said, "as you can see, this is a multi-artist show. Some of the talent is local, some from further afield. Many of the latter are old acquaintances whose work I like to display whenever I can. But one of my favorite painters is the Pixie Point Bay watercolorist Clio Hearst."

"Clio Hearst," Maris said, tilting her head. "I'm afraid I'm not familiar with her work."

"You are in the majority, but I would like to change that." Mikhail led her to a small grouping of almost photorealistic images. "I think you might be particularly interested in her work because of the subject matter." Smiling broadly, Mikhail turned back to Maris. "As you see, one of her favorite subjects might be familiar to you."

"Oh, my goodness," Maris exclaimed, "the lighthouse and B&B." The details in the attached two-story Victorian were positively lifelike. The many gables and traditional windows were accurate, as was the coloring. The conical white tower topped with its glass optics house glowed against a stunningly vibrant sunset. "She's really managed to capture the...spirit of the place." Maris had to smile to herself, since the Old Girl actually did have a spirit. She regarded Mikhail. "They're absolutely beautiful. I can definitely see why she's one of your favorites."

Mikhail nodded. "A local artist who makes the most of the local environment." He gestured to the nearby paintings. "These are all part of her Coastside Series."

Maris stepped closer and peered at the images of the bay and the pier. Tide pools seemed to brim with life, and the Pixie Point Bridge dramatically spanned a canyon on the coast. But no matter the subject, tiny brush strokes in their hundreds, maybe even thousands, created a vivd impression that seemed to surpass real life.

"These are remarkable," she said.

"Please excuse us," someone said from behind.

Maris and Mikhail turned to see Minako

and Alfred Page, the owners of the bookstore and hosts for the evening's gala. They were both holding platters of delicious looking *hors d'oeuvres*.

"May I offer you some warm salmon shumai," Minako said, pointing to it, "also vegetable spring rolls, butternut squash with gouda pot stickers, and hand rolls of spicy yellowtail sushi."

"You certainly may," Maris said, taking a small paper plate and napkin from the tray. "Minako, you've really outdone yourself."

The diminutive Asian store owner beamed at her, her sleek black hair swaying as she bobbed her head. "Thank you," she said. "We also have some liquid refreshments."

"Japanese whisky and sake," Alfred said, holding his tray forward. It was covered in little ceramic sake glasses of all shapes and colors, some with amber liquid, and some with clear. The heady scent of the alcohol mixed nicely with the aromatic smell of the warm food.

Mikhail selected a shot of whisky. "Thank you," he said, and lifted the little glass to both of them. "And thank you again for hosting the gala. You have done a magnificent job."

As one of the largest establishments in Pixie Point Bay, Maris was hard-pressed to think of another place that could have hosted it. Certainly there was no other that could have done it with as much style.

"I'll try these scrumptious delights to begin with," she said as she chose the salmon shumai and the spicy yellowtail hand roll. Though she would have loved to take two of everything, her ongoing quest for lower cholesterol and weight loss stopped her. "Thank you."

"Truly," Alfred said smiling. "It's very much–"

"Our pleasure," Minako said.

Maris grinned at them as they resumed circulating among the guests. Though Alfred was of a medium height and build, he still towered over his petite wife. And with his blonde hair and bespectacled blue eyes, they couldn't have looked more different. But Maris couldn't think of another couple that she'd met that seemed so together.

As the warm salmon shumai melted in

her mouth, she detected a hint of scallion and ginger. The combination was perfect.

"Good, is it not?" Mikhail said smiling. Maris could only nod, as she enjoyed the tender texture and just the right amount of soy sauce seasoning. "I think I ate a whole tray during the setup. Minako and Alfred made everything themselves."

Maris covered her mouth with the napkin. "Wow," she muttered. She was going to have to see if they'd be willing to share the recipe.

"If you can stand my company for just another minute," Mikhail said, "may I introduce you to Clio?"

"Mmm," Maris said, nodding after she swallowed. "I'd love to meet her."

He glanced around the room. "Ah, there she is."

Maris followed him to a slim woman who appeared to be in her early thirties. Her auburn hair had been gathered and pinned behind her head and her bright blue eyes gazed at them as they approached. She was holding a tiny sake cup, and chatting with a few people. But as Mikhail approached, she excused herself and came forward to meet them.

"Maris Seaver," Mikhail said to her, "I would like you to meet the artist who painted the lovely photos of your lighthouse." He inclined his head to her. "Clio Hearst."

Clio's eyes widened and she smiled as she thrust out her hand. "You own the lighthouse?" she asked.

"I do," Maris said, shaking her hand.

"I absolutely adore it. It's one of my favorite subjects."

Maris glanced back at the artwork. "So I saw. And I must say, you've really managed to capture the magic of the place."

"Oh thank you," Clio said, glancing downward. "I hope I did it justice. But it's wonderful to hear you approve."

"How could she not?" Mikhail said. "But if you two ladies will excuse me, I think I might see a prospective buyer." He gave them a quick bow and hurried off.

Maris turned to the artist. "Really, all of your work is amazing. Not just the lighthouse —even if it's my favorite. I can see why Mikhail chose to feature you."

A little color rose to Clio's cheeks. "That's so kind of you. I–"

The sound of raised voices interrupted her. Maris turned to see Aurora Puddlefoot arguing heatedly with a well-dressed man that she recognized. Like Mikhail, art critic Langston Spaulding and his wife were guests at the B&B and had come for the express purpose of the art gala. But at the moment the artsy couple were being assailed by the owner of the town's gift store, Magical Finds.

• • • • •

Buy The Witch Who Filled in the Picture

FREE BOOK

If you'd like to learn how Maris arrived in Pixie Point Bay and got her start, you can read *The Witch Who Saw the Light* for FREE by signing up for my newsletter at the link below.

Get A Free Book

DEDICATION

For Mr. Bee's Knees

COPYRIGHT

Copyright © 2020 Emma Belmont

This is a work of fiction. Names, characters, places, and incidents are products of the author's imagination or are used fictitiously and are not to be construed as real. Any resemblance to actual events, locales, organizations, or persons, living or dead, is coincidental.

All rights reserved. No part of this book may be used or reproduced in any manner, stored in or introduced into a retrieval system, or transmitted, in any form, or by any means (electronic, mechanical, photocopying, recording, or otherwise), without the prior written consent of the copyright owner.

The scanning, uploading, and distribution of this book via the Internet or via any other means without the permission of the copyright owner is illegal. Please purchase only authorized electronic editions, and do not participate in or encourage electronic piracy of copyrighted materials. Your support of the author's rights is appreciated.